STRANGE AFFAIRS, GINGER HAIRS

ARTHUR GRIMESTEAD

Matador
9 Priory Business Park,
Wistow Road, Kibworth Beauchamp,
Leicestershire. LE8 0RX
Tel: 0116 279 2299
Email: books@troubador.co.uk
Web: www.troubador.co.uk/matador
Twitter: @matadorbooks

ISBN 978 1789018 110

British Library Cataloguing in Publication Data.
A catalogue record for this book is available from the British Library.

Printed and bound in Great Britain by 4edge Limited
Typeset in 11pt Adobe Jenson Pro by Troubador Publishing Ltd, Leicester, UK

Matador is an imprint of Troubador Publishing Ltd

To all who helped, heartfelt thanks.
To all who hindered, fuck you.

PART ONE

November 1998

One

*Hello good fella, are
you well my friend?*

I awoke, and my first thought was: *I'm going to kill myself.*

I wasn't desperate, I just couldn't be bothered to get out of bed.

Staring at the ceiling, I trailed my thoughts around a swirl of Artex. A minute passed, during which I did not die.

You see, I had a general fear of death; a fancy for melodrama; and it was signing-on day. If I couldn't be bothered to get out of bed, I probably couldn't be bothered to kill myself.

A woman gazed over me, pouting her silicone-enhanced lips. The poster of Page Three Lucy dominated my room – well worth the KitKat I swapped it for. Her breasts were captivating and always cheered me, albeit with a predictable transience.

I rolled over, reaching for a half depleted cola bottle. Just out of grasp, my finger tickled the label – I asked the cola genie for fewer spots, no holes in my underwear and the ability to be recognised by persons other than the Jobcentre staff. Indeed, I had to *be* there in an hour to mark the pinnacle of another vocation-less fortnight. My bed was calling me to hide under the duvet and pretend Lucy lay with me, but the sniff of money-for-nothing won out. Hastily, I pulled on yesterday's jeans and socks, encasing the stench of the latter in a pair of Three Stripe trainers. Then, collecting my dog-eared benefit book, I blew Lucy a kiss and set off to the land of the jobseeker.

I sat waiting for a number thirty-eight to take me into town. The bus shelter was shrunk to microscopic proportions under a looming tower block, somewhere at the top being my recently departed abode. As I looked up, the grey amalgamation of concrete ascended into the sky and seemed to infect Mother Nature with its greyness. The sun always seemed shy round our way. People walked as if they couldn't be bothered, hands in pockets and dragging along their feet – even the sprogs of the teenaged mothers seemed too lazy to cry.

Someone plonked down beside me. 'All right Ginger?'

I looked up.

'How's it goin'?'

It was Syd, a skinny weasel-like kid, who wore glasses so thick he could probably see into next week.

'Been up to owt?'

I shrugged my shoulders. 'Dunno really.'

'Where y'off now?'

'Sign on,' I grunted.

'Oh. Seen owt'a Wacko?'

'No.'

'I'm supposed to be meetin' 'im. I've got 'im one a these.' He pulled open a Kwik Save carrier, revealing a hoard of mobile phones and offering them like a bag of sweets. 'At least 'undred quid y'd pay at Carphone Ware'ouse. Y'can 'ave one for fifty?'

I grunted, shaking my head. 'I'm skint.'

'The world's moved on from carrier pigeon – get the fuck with it!' He snatched back the tangle of antennas, his tone nudging superior. 'I got on t'internet last week – gettin' porno piped in 24/7.'

I ignored him, though secretly I was jealous. 'So where did you get that lot?' I said, nodding towards his swag bag.

'Chip Shop Chas. 'e's got even more of 'em.'

I groaned. 'You back in with him?'

''e's all right Chas.'

'He's well dodgy.'

'I could get y'bit'a work with 'im. Make some proper wonga instead'a broodin' on dole.'

I gave a tut. 'No ta.'

'Suit yerself.' Syd lit a fag and inhaled as if it were his life support. 'Y'wun't know a good thing if it bit yer 'and off.'

'Everyone knows that chip shop's a front.'

'So what?'

So… nothing, absolutely nothing – it's not like I give a shit. I care more about the price of Tampax. I was quiet and gazed at the kerb.

'This time next year *y'll* still be signin' on,' said Syd, pointing his fag rather accusingly. 'While I'm signin' a big cheque for a big new Jag.'

'Yeh right.'

'I'm tellin' ye, Chas runs this estate. Every break-in, every two-'undred percent loan, it all goes back to 'im. But 'e's careful, y'see, and nothin' ever sticks. I mean, what else is there?'

'You could try being honest.'

Syd laughed.

'So everyone has to burgle houses for a living?' I snapped.

'Dunt everyone do that already?'

'*I* don't.'

He blew a lung full of smoke in my face. 'Y'know, even at school y'dint 'ave a clue.'

'I did better than *you*,' I spluttered.

'GCSE Astronomy? What does that qualify y'for? The Russell Grant fan club?'

I frowned. 'That's astrology.'

'Forget all that bollocks. Get a degree in life and the first thing y'll learn is y'don't get owt for nowt 'less y'go and take it.'

'What do *you* know about life? You're younger than me.'

'Enough not to be a miserable twat bag on dole.' He pulled out a wad of cash, waving it in my face. 'I've shifted twelve phones for Chas this week – twen'y percent for me – that's 'undred and twen'y quid.'

'Dirty money.'

'Only if y'wipe yer arse on it.'

I ignored him as my bus appeared – late as usual.

Syd held out a fiver. 'There y'go Ginger, treat yerself.'

A man of principle would have snubbed him, but five quid covered a Big Mac and a milkshake. I snatched it and stood up.

'See y'around then,' said Syd.

I said nothing and caught the bus to town.

'Can I see your job search log?' said Sandra, New Deal Personal Advisor.

'It's at home,' I said – the desk between us seemed like a judge's bench.

'You need to show your efforts to find work, Mr Jones.'

I offered a perfunctory glance towards the noticeboard, pointing at random. 'Can I apply for that one?'

'We encourage clients to apply for as many jobs as possible.'

'Right.'

Her tone dropped. 'Or face sanctions.'

As I sat opposing Sandra's pointy nose, I felt very dissatisfied with the way New Labour were making me jump through hoops for money – New Deal was a bad deal.

'Administrative Assistant, Choice Seafood,' said Sandra, reading from her computer screen. 'You'd like to make an application now?'

I shrugged. 'If you say so.'

She sniffed, fidgeted in her seat and then continued to read. 'Do you have previous experience within a busy office environment?'

'No.'

'Are you computer literate?'

'Not really.'

'Qualifications?'

'Kind of.'

Her French tips gave an exaggerated wrap over the enter key and her nose returned to pointing in my direction. 'I've arranged an interview for you, next Thursday 10.30am.'

My stomach seemed to capsize. 'What?'

'A New Deal placement is a gateway into employment,' she said, smiling. 'Often, no experience is necessary.'

'But I'm busy next week.'

'I could refer your case to a decision maker, Mr Jones. But that could mean sanctions.'

'Right.'

'Anything else we can do for you today?'

'I need to sign on,' I mumbled, offering my benefit book.

'Well, I'm breaking for lunch right now, so if you'd like to re-join the queue and wait for one of my colleagues…'

I dragged myself up, pulling a face, and mooched to the back of the queue.

Two

*I could have been the
mayor, the lord, the king.*

I stood outside a bogey green door, flushed and a little out of breath. Scraped into the paint was the number 52 – someone had nicked the brass digits and sold them to number 25. Bracing myself, I opened the door.

'I'm back!'

There was no reply.

In the living room, obesity anchored Dad to his armchair. He didn't look up from the telly.

So, I ignored him and mooched through to the kitchen. There I found Mum over the hob, sucking on a stub of Silk Cut. She looked at me hard, her long greying hair pulled back and her forehead shining. 'I'm doing Dad's dinner first – *you'll* have to wait.'

A sausage spat at her, she flipped it, coughed and seasoned the food with spittle. Hunger was never really satisfied in our home, just battered into submission.

Returning to the living room, I could remember what we'd had for dinner all that week by looking at the stains on Dad's shirt.

'Where you been ugly git?' he said.

'Jobcentre.'

He grunted. Some design programme had a greater command for his attention, and I watched with him for a moment. I wondered what Carol Smillie would make of our flat – considering Mum's forty-a-day habit had colour co-ordinated everything a strange brown that, if you scratched it, stuck beneath your fingernails.

'A woman from Social's coming to see Dad later,' shouted Mum from the kitchen.

'What for?' I said.

'Ask Dad – they sent him a letter.'

Dad frowned. 'Checking I'm not working on the side. It's an insult.'

'You *are* working on the side,' I said.

'Na – don't count if it's a matter of survival. Anyway, a bit of bootlegged baccy never hurt anyone.'

In 1970, Dad had had to give up a career in forklift truck operation because of a bad leg. While on a break he'd attacked a vending machine that refused to supply him a Pepsi. The result was a broken toe, which then became arthritic – sufficient disability for him to live off state benefit for the rest of his life.

Mum went on: 'So you're staying in. I've got a longer shift at chip shop again.'

This was cause for complaint. 'What do *I* have to be here for?'

'I'm supposed to be laid up,' said Dad. 'You've got to do things for me.'

'Like what?'

His stomach wobbled as he raised his voice. 'Everything, owt to do with benefits and I'm an invalid. I'm not giving it back to that grinning-shit-face Blair.'

I looked away. 'As if I've got nothing better to do.'

'You never have anything better to do – you're a lazy sod.'

I kept quiet as Mum brought him his dinner.

'And speaking of which,' said Mum, settling a lap tray across Dad's legs. 'Your board's going up.'

'What?' I blurted.

'Eighty,' she said.

Dad smiled at his food. 'Only fair.'

'I can't afford—'

'No-one ever gave *us* charity,' said Mum.

'Nope,' said Dad. 'Get a lodger if we need to.'

'No way!'

Dad appeared more concerned with his sausages. 'Bit well done aren't they?'

Mum sniffed, trudging back towards the kitchen. 'Mary never came home again last night,' she mumbled.

'A right little tart that one's turned into,' said Dad.

My voice gave a disbelieving squeak. 'So you're kicking me out?'

'Pay your way, no problem,' said Dad.

'I'll stay with friends,' I snapped.

He was enticed to look up from his food. 'What bloody friends?'

This was a fair point – I'd always known grassing-up the Year Ten amyl nitrate incident would come back to haunt me. Also, I could have been more sympathetic when John Southwick started chemotherapy – but he never did give back my copies of *Fiesta* magazine.

Dad squeezed a bottle of HP as if it were for stress relief – the top burst and turned his fry up into a plate of brown sludge. 'Bollocks! I'm not eating *that*.' He gestured with his cutlery. 'Here, *you* have it.'

'I don't like brown sauce. It tastes like battery acid,' I said.

'Guess you'll go hungry then won't you.'

I pulled a face, hunger enticing me to take the plate and chance a taste. With a bent fork, I stabbed a sausage and dived in with a chomp. My God it was horrible. I dropped the plate onto Dad's lap tray, my stomach retching.

Dad cringed. 'Give over. I can't hear the telly.'

'I can't eat this,' I said through a splutter.

'Then make yourself bloody useful for once – go make me a cuppa.' He held out a mug which stated he was 'too sexy for his tea.'

'And who'll make the tea if you evict me?' I snapped.

'Mum's not going anywhere. Anyway, what's an extra twenty?'

'*Everything* I get!'

Dad shrugged. 'Times are hard.'

I snatched his mug, kicking my feet into the kitchen. Mum was quiet as I prepared a concoction of teapot dregs, globs of sour milk and sugar – warmed a little in the microwave. Returning a minute later, Dad gestured petulantly for me to rest the drink on the coffee table. I obeyed as the doorbell sounded with a short jingling blast of the theme from *Happy Days*.

'Door!' said Dad.

Again, I obeyed, answering to the fresh face of a very pretty lady.

'Hi,' she said brightly. 'I'm Carla Penny from the Department of Social Security. You had a letter?'

The lady fitted into an oversized trouser suit rather awkwardly, her blouse slightly low cut and her cleavage making me feel warm below the waist. 'Er...'

'May I come in?'

I held the door open and she entered with unassuming steps, perhaps unappreciative of my attention to her jiggly bits. I nodded towards the living room, following behind.

'Mr Jones?' she said.

Dad took a moment to switch his gaze from the telly, grunting as he gave her a look over, lazily, as though she wasn't a person at all, but a very long form that he couldn't be bothered to fill in. He then grunted at me and talked past her. 'What's going on? Who's this?'

'I'm Carla Penny from the Department of Social Security,' said the lady, sidestepping back into Dad's eyeline. 'I'm here a little earlier than planned, but I was already in the neighbourhood and I thought… How are you?'

Dad frowned and looked back at the telly. 'Be a lot better without *you* sneaking up on me.'

'Perhaps if I'm interrupting lunch, I could… Er—'

'Go buy a watch and learn to tell the time?'

'Sit down,' I said, my amicable tone eliciting a smile from the lady and helping to temper the mood. She glanced around, tentatively, and settled on the edge of the settee. As she fumbled in her bag, a slight tremor to her hand betrayed one of two things: a) she had early Parkinson's Disease; or b) she was a rookie. A quick wink from Dad confirmed that he too had clocked her.

The lady settled, sitting with a clipboard on her lap and looking up at Dad. 'Now, do you know why I'm here Mr Jones?'

He didn't reply.

'I've been seconded to the Hull branch to head a new home visit scheme—'

'Ull!' said Dad.

'Pardon.'

'The 'Ull branch. Silent H and a capital U.' He pulled a face at me. 'God help us if she can't even speak proper.'

'Right, well… It's a scheme to visit the long term disabled such as yourself to—'

'I'm not bloody cheating,' said Dad indignantly.

'Pardon?'

'You heard me.'

'No-one's saying that you are Mr Jones.'

'I hope not.'

Mum plodded into the room, exchanging Dad's soiled sausages for a plateful of freshly cooked. She glanced across to the lady, gave a tut and rolled her eyes. Dad was sprightly with his first chomp, oblivious to the universe outside as he slobbered over his food like a pig being fattened for market day. Mum turned away, and as she returned to the kitchen I imagined her expression somewhere between resignation and imminent vomit.

'So,' I said to the lady, loudly, as much concerned with counteracting the sound of Dad eating. 'What *would* be cheating exactly? Maybe a lodger? Paying rent?'

She fidgeted in her seat. 'Perhaps, but I'm not here to...'

Glancing across the room, Dad's face had reddened and seemed to be inflating, a blocked vent by way of a mouth stuffed with sausages.

I smiled and continued: 'What about selling bootlegged tobacco? Is *that* classed as cheating?'

The lady looked puzzled. 'I'm not sure if...'

A hideous choking sound commanded our attention, our heads turned in unison as Dad spat half a sausage with such force it projected aloft the coffee table, descended like an incendiary bomb and hit the lady clean between the eyes.

'Any baccy that comes in this flat is for my own personal use!' bawled Dad. 'You can't prove otherwise!'

The lady recoiled into her seat, her hand tremulous as she wiped gravy from her forehead. 'Well I really don't see what that has to do with me.'

'I'll tell you right now – stop my benefit and there'll be hell to pay.'

'But I'm not here to,' she said, almost pleadingly.

But Dad had stopped listening and his outrage turned to me. 'And *you'd* better toe the line,' he said, pointing a finger that appeared to have the contents of a plant pot stuck beneath the nail. 'Stop being a clever little shit or I'll kick you out so quick your arse won't hit the carpet.'

'Alright, calm—'

Dad screamed and grasped his leg.

'Mr Jones?'

'Get me pills. Quick!' he wailed.

The lady was visibly shaken. 'What's wrong?'

'You've upset his arthritis,' I said.

'I've only been here a minute.'

'It's very sensitive to stress.'

'But...'

I found Dad's medication and mooched over, muttering into his ear. 'Who'll bring the pills if you evict me?'

Dad writhed, but fighting the agony, he struggled to get a pill down.

'Deep breaths Dad – you'll be fine,' I said, exaggerating the sentiment.

'What can I do?' said the lady.

'I think you'd better go.'

'Should I call a doctor?'

'Just leave us alone. You've done enough already.'

She looked on, distraught as Dad voiced his pain. Her top lip wobbled, then as Dad began to pray, she mumbled an apology and made a prompt, rather flustered collection of her effects.

'Perhaps we should arrange a more, er, convenient time,' she said.

Soon, we heard the door slam and Dad sat up. 'Job well done. Fish and chips tonight!' he said, tossing his pills away nonchalantly.

'I'm fed up of this. You know they'll catch you one day.'

Dad smirked and took a sip of his special tea – I smiled as he was nearly sick.

Three

Three large gins
and I got you.

That evening, a waft of fish carried through the flat, tickling my nasal hair with the most delightful smell. Fish and chips was a rare treat, arousing such excitement that I pounced on Mum as she entered the living room with two steaming bags.

'Bloody gannet!' She gave me a clout.

Undeterred, I followed her into the kitchen. Mum piled three plates with fishes, chips, burgers, chicken – anything you could batter – golden mountains dripping in glorious grease.

Back in the living room, Dad moved quicker than I'd ever seen him as he sat up ready to eat. The heating was on full, *EastEnders* was on the telly and we sat and scoffed.

'Been thinkin', said Dad, aiming a brief, seemingly begrudging glance in my direction. 'Maybe we can call it eighteen extra, for the rent like.'

'Leaving me with two quid a fortnight?' *Big whoop, fatty.* 'What am I supposed to do with that?'

'You don't *do* nowt anyway.'

I was quiet. Self-analysis was a difficult process for me, literally by the fact that there was so little to analyse; and emotionally by the fact that what I *could* analyse was essentially turd. All I knew was that I wanted to be different, and I'd known it deep down and for so long the self-knowledge had started to eat me from the inside.

Dad sneered. 'Hardly grabbin' life by the short and curlies are you? More bloody life in my dirty socks.'

Indeed, I envied Dad's socks – they had a purpose. I mean, where would the world be without socks? Cold and covered in blisters. Where would the world be without me? Coping with a surplus of anti-dandruff shampoo.

I took a deep breath. 'But eighteen quid? Can't you just...'

Dad grinned, flashing crooked, mustard and occasionally absent teeth. 'Offer bloody withdrawn.'

For a few disturbing seconds, I looked at him and saw myself peering back – dull eyes, a bobble on his nose that could have guided Santa's sleigh. A shiver trickled down my back. Thirty years on, with my own grey hair, I could see myself fitting easily into those mucky clothes that seemed to hang on him with indolence. I mean, in eighteen years I'd accomplished nothing but a large collection of smutty magazines.

'I've put fish and chips on your slate,' said Mum. 'Ten pound thirty-seven.'

Dad spluttered, it sounding like a convulsion. 'What?'

'Stop choking Morris!'

'Giro's not 'til next Tuesday! I can't bloody afford that.'

I looked at Mum. Cigarettes had destroyed the decade between her and Dad – bordering forty, her crinkled top lip could have been used as a bus pass. 'Well, how much extra you getting from that lady?' she said. 'I'm sure that'll cover it.'

'I told you,' said Dad, looking away. 'We got rid of her before she tried to *stop* my bloody benefit.'

'Well they went to see Barry the other day – you know, him with the gout – and he's getting ten quid extra every week now. It's not fair if other people are getting more.'

Dad poked at his fish and chips. 'Ten pound thirty-seven? Is that what my life's worth? Cos you know what Chas does when people don't settle.'

'Don't talk silly Morris!'

'He'll just have to dock *your* wages – otherwise it'll be *me* that gets battered, never mind the bloody fish.'

Mum gave a tut. 'Where's that letter?' Her legs dangled from beneath her lap tray, overreaching for the coffee table, the strain accentuated the veins in her stick-thin calves. She snatched an envelope, squinting as she passed it to me. '*You'll* have to read it.'

I obliged, and after reading the first few lines, offered an unrestrained smirk. 'It says here that there's a "new home visit scheme to inform the long term disabled of a new legislation that may result in an increase of the benefits you receive".'

Dad dropped his cutlery. 'What? What does that mean?'

It means you're a fat fuck who's just shit-out. 'Dunno,' I said.

He pointed at Mum. '*You* read it.'

'I've not got my spectacles, Morris.'

'Give it here!' he snapped.

Unwilling to shift from beneath my lap tray, I folded the letter into a concord-like thing and tossed it at Dad – it stuck upright in his mushy peas.

Dad began to read, groaning almost painfully. The focus of his annoyance was me. 'Your board'll have to be an extra *thirty* to make up for this.'

'You can't do that,' I shouted, indignation forcing me to gasp for air.

'Just *done* it.'

My eyes scanned over the room, scouting for support. *That coffee table's pretty inanimate, that cushion's not going to say anything. Hmm. Guess it'll have to be…* 'Mum! Tell him.'

Mum glanced over each of us, then shrugged.

'Going for a bloody walk!' said Dad.

A walk? You barely moved when the first floor was on fire.

Dad's overhang sagged as he stood, grabbed a magazine from the coffee table and wrapped a piece of fish. 'Off down The Eagle,' he grumbled.

'Morris,' Mum croaked. 'You can't take your tea down the pub. Not in the *TV Times!*'

It was quiet for a moment, broken as the front door slammed behind Dad.

'Don't know what to think of him sometimes,' said Mum. 'If it hadn't've been for the twinkle in his eye and his few years' extra experience...' She appeared wistful, gazing down over her fish. 'Well there'd be no *you*, for a start. *And* I'd have kept dancing.'

At one point in her life, Mum could have been described as a dancer, loosely. She'd been spotted dancing in clubs in the 1970s, which, cutting-out a few blow jobs, led to being one fifth of a troupe that once filled in for Diana Ross on *Top of the Pops*. When she became pregnant – with me – it was decided that she shouldn't jiggle about so much. Apparently, I ended her career.

'Can't you have a word with Dad? About the board?' I said, refusing to acknowledge her age old gripe.

'Not up to me,' she snapped. 'Eat your tea.'

'But...' I pulled a face and scoffed. It wasn't often I could enjoy decent food in abundance, and I took some solace as my teeth skewered the fish, an out-squelching of grease dripping from my chin and back down to the plate – it was a strange pleasure, until mid-chew my teeth caught something tough, enough to send a twinge along my jaw. My reflex was to spit the mouthful, then probe the glob of fish flakes with my finger. A moment later, I was baffled to find myself holding a ring. It hardly seemed real, but there it was resting on the palm of my hand – and not a bad ring at that. It was gold and had a large red stone that glimmered through the grease.

It seemed a catalogue job – I couldn't think of anyone who could afford more – but I reckoned it could be worth a couple of quid.

'What's that?' said Mum, squinting. 'A ring? What *you* doing with a ring?'

Fortune had a habit of avoiding me, so I lied. 'Bit of junk from a Christmas cracker,' I said, nodding to my plate. 'Was in that fish.'

Mum frowned, checking her fingers. 'Well it's not mine.'

'I should sue the chip shop.'

Her eyes widened, seemingly in recognition of said fish being battered by her own hand – making her perfectly blameworthy. 'You can't. I need that job. Your board would have to double... *treble.*'

I beheld the ring and shrugged. 'Maybe I don't care. Maybe I'll bugger off anyway.'

'What? Where?'

Hmm, where indeed. Maybe having friends isn't such an overrated concept after all... Maybe I could get fifty quid for this ring? 'Anywhere. I could get enough for a fare to London.'

Mum laughed though her nose, the blast of air seeming nervous, yet annoyingly condescending. 'You're not Dick Wittington.'

This was true, but I *was* Ginger Jones and I could do what the hell I wanted. 'But what's to stop me eh?'

She sniffed, and all conversation diminished as she lit a fag and drowned the room with her clogged breathing.

To lose a ring in a haddock seemed a bizarre act of carelessness – how, why and *who* the hell? But it belonged to me now, finders keepers and all that. Indeed, I promised myself that tomorrow I'd be down the pawn shop trading my auspicious find for an auspicious future. With fifty quid I could do just about anything! A strange feeling crept over me, bright and tingling.

It was optimism.

Four

It's plain you're insane
to live a life so sad.

I thought hard that night. A ring could bring cash, and cash could bring the means to actually *do* something. It sounded simple enough, and so the following day brought an early start – even before Kilroy. I knew of a Buy, Swap or Sell shop round the back of town. My granddad had died a couple of months before and Grandma had flogged his gold tooth there, so I reckoned you could get rid of just about anything.

English Street stood a strongman's spit from the River Humber. The main road and side-shoots offered a mismatch of industrial buildings, contemporary steel units sitting amongst the spalling bricked relics of a fishing industry. Warehouses had been chopped-up and repurposed by low-level business – *cut price MOTs; belly busting full English; authentic Tai massage; cheap rehearsal space (with PA!)*. Yet despite these amazing deals, there was a gloomy solitude to the streets, of the kind endemic to areas of dying industry.

Several strides along a cobbled side-street, I found the low-level business I required. From outside, the place was intimidating. The whole shop was caged under a thick steel mesh, a red neon sign flickered in the window and a few dead letters obscured the message somewhat: Go-d- bo-g-- and so-d -or -ash.

I ventured inside.

A bell heralded my entrance, though the shop was very still. I stood amongst a poky medley of miscellanea – videos to violins, pocket phones to pocket nasal hair removers; the most eye catching thing a collection of prosthetic limbs hanging above the counter. As I observed more closely, a man with a wart on his chin appeared, like a genie.

'Hello. How can I help? Are you interested in a leg?'

'Er... No,' I said, a little startled. 'A ring.'

'Rings?' He pointed to a glass case display.

'No, I mean I want to sell a ring.'

'Right.' He rubbed his wart thoughtfully. He was short and wore a tight blue cagoule that clung to his paunch – I couldn't help but imagine him as a garden gnome. 'Well, you'd better give us a shifty,' he said.

I passed a matchbox, which he slipped open to find the swag wrapped in some cotton wool.

Examining through an eye lens, he held the ring to the light. 'Very nice. Very nice. Where did you get this?'

I'd prepared a lie earlier that morning. 'It's, er, my sister's. She was engaged but she broke it off.'

The man took a deep breath. 'I'd need some proof of ownership first.'

'Like what?'

'Receipt. Insurance.'

'Well...' *Will chip paper do?* 'You know my grandma. She sold you a gold tooth not long ago.'

'Are you Hetty's grandlad?'

'Yeh.'

'Well I never. It's a pleasure to meet any one of the Joneses.' Following his lead, we shook hands. 'I knew your granddad really well. Wasn't it heart trouble?'

I shrugged. 'Dunno really… So, you want the ring?'

He appeared pensive, scrunching one eye and scrutinising the ring again. 'Your sister's?'

'Yeh.'

'Where'd she get it?'

'Her boyfriend.'

'Where'd *he* get it?'

'Dunno. Argos I think.'

The man looked back, holding me with a glare and pointing below the counter with a finger that looked like a cocktail sausage. 'If that's true – I've got a foot long todger.'

The doorbell heralded a young woman, struggling with a kid in a buggy. 'Hiya Arthur,' she said to the man. 'You all right?'

I reached for the ring, the man snatched back, flinching repeatedly as he placed the swag into the matchbox and tucked it down into his pocket. 'Best leave this with me, son,' he said, rearranging his face into a more affable presentation and hobbling to the woman's assistance. 'I'm not too bad luv,' he said with a fresh voice. 'What can I do you for?'

Just like at school, when: 'Sir! *Alex Turnbull nicked my dinner money.*'

'Idle bastard lost on the dogs again,' said the woman. 'I need to raise thirty quid for the rent – but I only got the buggy.'

'*Grow a spine, Jones. Stand up straight and go take it back.*'

'Let's have a shifty then,' said the man.

'*But sir—*'

The man bent over to inspect her offering, rubbing his back and sucking a gasp of air through his teeth.

'*Grow a spine, Jones.*'

I selected a prosthetic leg from above the counter, grasped the ankle and clobbered the man over the back of his head. He slumped into the buggy, dentures spilling over the baby.

'Oh my God! Help!' the woman screeched. 'He's trying to eat Charlene!'

I ignored her, frisked the man for my matchbox and ran away to find another buyer.

Three hours, seven miles and an igloo-like blister later, I realised off-loading the ring wasn't going to be that easy. I visited a handful of places – a dirty dive, a slightly less tawdry jeweller and three subtle shades in-between; of which two people asked me for proof of ownership, two told me to fuck off and one person produced a roll of cling-film and asked for a sexual favour. Aching and annoyed, I made my way home.

It was by The Pork Café that I met Syd, looking quite dapper in a shiny leather coat. He was going in for his dinner, 'It's a lovely steak pie in 'ere,' and asked me to tag along – I accepted when he offered to pay.

'Y'like the coat then?' he said, as we made ourselves comfortable in smokers' corner.

'It's all right,' I grunted.

'Guess 'ow much.'

'Dunno.'

'Go on, guess.'

'Fifty?'

''igher.'

'Eighty?'

''*igher.*'

'How should *I* know how much it cost?'

He grinned wider than a post box. 'Three-'undred and fifty notes. Double breasted, silk linin' – y'won't see anyone round 'ere wearin' one.'

He appeared overly chuffed with his clobber, disgustingly so, and I couldn't help but frown. As such, awkwardness lingered for a moment, the radio offering a chance for the *Spice Girls* to yell *'spice up your life.'* I reckoned I'd have preferred a less radical salt-and-vinegaring up of my life.

'I've been away for a couple a days,' said Syd, pausing to light a fag. 'Me and two other lads went up Leeds way to sort somert for Chas.'

'What?'

'Can't say – but it paid well.' He looked down on his coat and grinned. 'Ever been to Otley?'

Prat. You're a tragic prat.

'Chas 'as been well pissed off since I got back though.'

'Really,' I said, preoccupied.

'Yeh. It's been bad. Pigs turned up at 'is 'ouse yesterd'y mornin' – went through everythin' and left it a right shit tip.'

I wonder if Syd can flog the ring for me?

''e got wind of it beforehand like and got a package down to Leon at chip shop...'

Naa. I'd probably have to give him a cut.

'But when they cun't find nowt at 'is 'ouse, they went down the shop. Leon's changin' the oil and shits 'imself. Chucks a grand's worth a whizz in the fryer...'

Still, I don't mind spending a penny to pick up a pound.

'Then the pigs search Leon and find some wackie. They're already pissed off cos they've got nowt on Chas – so they cart 'im off instead. When word gets out, it's too late, yer old lady's opened up the shop and she's fryin' away, servin' whizz and chips to anyone who wants it, and Chas's got visions of little old ladies bombin' 'bout like... well like they're on fuckin' whizz.'

I laughed an arse crawler's laugh.

'But get this: it turns out that in the panic 'e'd got ridda the wrong package. The other stuff's safe and sound and the pigs'd gone straight past it! Bone idle. Only now he's missin' a couple a so called "personal items".'

'What?'

'An anniversary present or somert – I was too busy tryin' to get out of 'is way. 'e was cheesed off I can tell y'that.'

Syd sucked on his fag and paused to enjoy the hit of nicotine. It seemed a good moment to ask.

'Listen,' I said, a little coy. 'Do you reckon you can do us a favour?'

He smirked at me. 'Y'after some more mags? I've only got a few, but y'can 'ave 'em all for a fiver – some a the pages a stuck together.'

I felt my face flush. 'No. Can you flog something for us?'

'What?'

Under the table, discretely, I pulled the matchbox from my jeans pocket.

'That was it!' he blurted. 'I remember now – it was a ring.'

I looked puzzled.

'One with a fuck-off ruby in it.'

'Eh?'

'What Chas's lost. It was 'is mam's fortieth weddin' present. I remember now, 'e was rantin' 'bout it's the only thin' 'e's got left of 'er.'

The world seemed to pause as my thoughts scattered, danced about and regrouped at about the point of me understanding where my ring had come from.

'Mind,' said Syd, 'I 'eard she was a right old witch – she used to whack 'im with a big stick – I mean y'd think 'e'd wanna forget.'

I panicked, clasped the matchbox inside my fist and sat with my heart beating like someone was trying to get out from inside me.

'Whoever's got it won't 'ave any use for a ring anyway – not after Chas's chopped their fingers off.' Syd grinned, either through jest or sadistic pleasure: fear was tampering with my perception. 'Any'ow, what's this thingy y'want me to price up?'

'Nothing!' I said shortly.

'What's up?'

'Nowt. I've just... er... changed my mind.' I pushed the matchbox down to the deepest depths of my pocket, visions of bloody injuries creeping up on me, panic blurring any clear thoughts. 'So what's next?' I said, with as much composure as I could grasp.

Syd peered, sucking a breath through his teeth. 'Well the word's out. It'll turn up sooner or later, or when someone's 'ad a kickin'.'

I jumped to my feet. 'I've gotta go now.'

'Yer pie's on its way.'

'You know how it is. Things to do.'

'I've already paid for it.'

'Soz.'

Hurrying out, I clattered into a full tray of food – I didn't stop to make sense of the waitress's cursing.

Five

I am the king of
your pitiful life.

There was only one place I could flee – where Bovril was a beverage and the people could flatulate the theme tune to *Coronation Street* – there just wasn't anywhere else.

When I barged in, Dad was slumped in the living room and snoring like a fog horn. My entrance provoked little more than a snort and a flicker from the telly. I wanted him to wake up and bellow at me what to do in his spectacularly arrogant way; I wanted Mum to abandon her fish frying and care about *me* instead of the price of twenty Silk Cut; and I wanted my sister to come home for once, simply to know she was there. I made straight for my room and curled up. I lay there, dwelling on this bloody ring, but my brain, baking in panic, wasn't at its most astute. Soon I was out of control, conjectures flying about, all coming to land on a picture of me getting my head kicked in.

A door slammed. The noise resonated and bounced off the bedroom walls – for a second it seemed I could actually see it. I heard mumbling, chunky footsteps passed through the hallway, and then a voice overwhelmed the flat with an abrasiveness that could have grated concrete:

'*Where is he?*'

I jolted, a pulse of fear turning my legs to jelly. Unsteadily, I ventured out into the hallway, the door to the living room stood half open, and as I stood back against the wall, a gap below the hinge afforded me a stealthy view of what lay behind.

'*Chas!*' Dad stared up from his chair, wide eyes glazed with fear. His usually ample mouth appeared lost for words. 'I, er…'

The figure looming over him was fat, face showing an unhealthy shade of red and teeth masticating an imaginary chunk of brick. Chas snorted, like a horse, catching hold of a Silver Jubilee tea cup that lived on the mantelpiece and smashing it across Dad's comb-over. 'To focus your mind, Morris.'

Dad gurned, clearly in pain, and gave a succession of quick nods that appeared perfunctory and in fear of the remaining mantelpiece display being dismantled via his head.

The front door stood not ten paces away, the hallway, strewn with discarded jackets and shoes, seemed negotiable with pussy footsteps. How to pass the living room incognito remained to be fathomed – that is, after I'd finished fathoming: *Whose fucking great idea was it to come back to this shit hole?* And: *I'm Fucked.*

Back in the living room, Chas's attention was distracted by a photograph on the wall. He seemed to recognise the scene despite years of sunlight having faded the image to a haze. 'Well, well,' he said dourly. He yanked the frame, taking it from the wall and using a handkerchief to wipe away years of absent housekeeping . '1965, we won the cup. How old were we then? Fifteen?'

It was a picture of Dad as a snotling, standing proud in a line-up of West Hull Boys RL team.

Chas pointed someone out. 'There I am – prop. I got a pounding that season.'

Prop was very apt. He was built like a beer barrel – short and inclining outwards towards the middle. Despite his neatly fitting suit, I could easily imagine him brawling in a scrum.

'Funny eh, what life deals out?' Chas forced half a grin that was blatantly insincere. 'Here we are, thirty-odd years on, me now a successful businessman and you…' He glanced around our minging abode. 'Well, you know what I mean.'

For a second, I thought I saw a flash of shame cross Dad's eyes. 'Look, about that couple of quid I owe you, I can pay next week. But I'm skint see. It's our lass's fault.'

Chas held the photograph aloft, stretching enough to flash his girth, then expediting said portrait towards Dad's head. He diverted at the final millisecond, the frame splitting as he dropped it onto the carpet and released a laugh from deep within his belly. Dad remained rigid, fingernails clinging to the chair arm – he seemed nonplussed as he joined in Chas's mirth.

Chas stopped laughing, of a sudden, and I saw a second man step out from the kitchen. The man filled the doorway and cast such a shadow over the room I could have mistaken him for an eclipse – he was colossal. As he stepped forward, a bald head radiated pink in the light, I saw no beard, no tash, not even eyebrows, there wasn't a strand of hair on his whole head. His presence evoked a whimper from Dad. At once, I knew who the man must be.

He was The Slap.

The relationship was well fabled – two young outcasts who had found solace in each other's misery: Chas had moved from the opposite side of Hull, from a rival school and superior rugby team, while The Slap was a big, quiet lad afflicted with a peculiar condition which left him with not one fibre of hair on his whole body. They were both bullied viciously. As legend had it, the two of them jumped the local pools collector, a cantankerous old git who'd been doing the round for years. He gave a struggle and refused to hand over any cash, so The Slap showed no compunction in kicking it out of him – the old man died of his injuries shortly after. Such violence sent the shits up people, no-one would dare be a grass, and this marked the beginning of Chas's rise to tinpot villain. The Slap, however, practically vanished. Time passed and he was exaggerated to the point of mythical beast – a sighting of him became an event in itself. Most people, including me, reckoned he was just an imaginary friend of which Chas had failed to outgrow.

But not so, since I found myself staring at this great Tonka truck of a man. Still and silent, his poise was almost austere. I fidgeted, began to pant, as though desperate for a piss. I could think only to hide, shutting myself inside the junk cupboard, crouching, hands smothering my breathing. My ear pressed against the back of the cupboard, with such force I could hear my blood flow, the room behind muffled.

'Last time, Morris,' said Chas. 'Where's your lad?'

Dad blurted a reply: 'Went out. This morning. Not seen him. Honest.'

'When's he back?'

'Dunno. Really. I don't.'

'Is he a good boy, Morris? Keeps out of trouble?'

Dad sounded bemused. 'I, er, well suppose...'

'A very personal item of mine was taken yesterday.' I thought I could hear Chas's teeth grind. 'Something very dear to me.'

'Sorry about that, very sorry,' Dad mumbled.

'It belonged to Ma – a gift from Dad on their fortieth wedding anniversary. He passed away two months later. Now Ma's gone as well and it's the only thing I have left to remember her by.'

'But how can *I* help mate – I mean, well, it's not like, I mean, it's not got owt to do with me.'

'This personal item is a ring, Morris – a very expensive ring. And I have it on good authority that *Hetty Jones's grandlad* was down Arthur Longie's shop this morning trying to get rid of it.'

The absoluteness of Chas's voice seemed to delay Dad's reply, as he perhaps took time to reflect. 'But he's a dickhead.'

'A dickhead who's got my fucking ring.'

Anxiety forced my leg to twitch, striking a shelf, then toppling a miniature Christmas tree – a reactionary leg split to catch said decoration spread me over the cupboard floor like a Ginger Jones pâté.

'So you'd better hope you get to your son before we do,' said Chas. 'And now he's been warned, if I find he's flogged my ring to some dirty little Del Boy, I won't be responsible for what happens. Do you understand me?'

'Yeh. I understand Chas,' said Dad. 'Crystal clear.'

The front door slammed.

'What the bloody hell's going on in here?' said Mum.

'Hello Eileen,' said Chas.

'What's happened?'

'A slight accident I'm afraid.'

'Just keep your gob shut woman,' said Dad.

Mum's voice rose an octave. 'I've had that cup for years – it's a limited edition. Now look at the state of it! Is this what I get for finishing a hard shift?'

Dad sounded panicky. 'Give over woman. What the hell you doing?'

'Fixing it!'

Footsteps stomped out into the hall, vibrating through me. A second later the cupboard door swung open. Mum stared, then a thud as I dropped the miniature Christmas tree. There was a tube of super glue in an old biscuit tin, which I offered to her, miming in earnest for her to keep quiet – but it was like trying to silence an air-raid siren.

She hollered at me. 'What you doing in here, idiot?'

I didn't hesitate to flee the cupboard, Mum withering into a heap as I shoved her aside. I made flight for the front door, negotiating the mess in the hall like a game of hopscotch. Out on the landing, seconds passed in an eternity, the lift unresponsive to my desperate button prods. The Slap was soon behind, followed closely by Chas, and they came for me like a freight train.

'I want my ring!' balled Chas. 'You can't run – I'll *always* find you.'

His threat hung in the air – I thought better of waiting for the lift. So to the stairwell, twenty-six flights, down, down, down, feet pounding up the rear. Fear kept me going like a Duracell battery, on and on and on. Ground level appeared a couple of fry-ups short of heart failure, but still on and on and on. Out into the estate, without direction, I shoved my way through school kids larking football, down a side passage, palpitations revving when I saw nothing in front but—

Brick wall.

The ground seemed to shake under The Slap's pursuit – I had no choice but to shin it. A running jump, I grabbed on, kicking my legs furiously. The Slap charged, trench coat streaming – in a second I was pinned by my throat. I froze, as if he were a grizzly bear and I was pretending to be dead. With his face pressed close, I saw the imperfections were vast, an accident of God's hobby as a panel beater. He kept so silent, but with a fixed scowl that commanded surrender.

'OK. Let go,' said Chas, his voice scraping along the passage. The Slap obeyed, I cowered as The Chip Shop King strolled over, sweating, his suit ruffled.

'Where is it?' he said.

I gazed up, resigned to my fate.

'I said *where is it?*'

'I-i-in my pocket.' I fumbled over my jeans with jelly hands.

'Do you think I'm a fool, eh? A clown here to entertain you?'

'I'm sorry—'

'Someone should teach you a lesson – the way *I* had to learn.' I caught my reflection in his eyes and it seemed to distort with a glimmer of anger. 'My ma had a stick for when I misbehaved, three lashes on the bones of my arse. She was a vicious bitch. Your daddy was liberal with his fists too; until I was big enough to hit back. You never forget a good beating, it's character building.' He prodded me with a stumpy finger – his scorn was palpable. 'And I want to see how much character *you've* got.'

Fear grasped control of me and triggered a knee-jerk reaction. My leg twitched, jabbed up and caught Chas clean between the legs. A cringe-making yelp reverberated and he jack-knifed, clinging to his bollocks. As he staggered back, his boot clipped a dustbin, he lost his feet and hit the ground like a giant sack of King Edwards.

Everything was then very still. Chas sprawled over the concrete, face down amongst teabags, spaghetti bolognaise and various other contents of a dustbin – but he was breathing, so presumably wasn't dead. The Slap moved in, narrow eyes moving between the slumped sack of villainy and myself.

'It was an accident. I'm sorry!' I blurted.

He knelt beside Chas, prodding for a trace of consciousness, and I imagined the Chip Shop King to be some kind of mother ship, without which all minions had begun to malfunction.

'An ambulance. I can call an ambulance,' I said, clasping my hands to disguise the tremor. 'Have you got a mobile?'

The Slap remained still, silent. His hand clenched, jerking towards me, then still again. A second surge saw him remove his trench coat and cover Chas – as a robotic arm upholstering a car seat.

'There's a pub in the next street, I could run there and—'

A gate opened further along the passage, a man in overalls puffing on a cigarette as he guided a bicycle through. He stared, taking a good drag and then a protracted exhalation. 'What's going on here?'

'There's been an accident,' I said, the words pouncing. 'Can I use your phone?'

The Slap extended his legs – like hydraulic cylinders raising him to full brick shithouse. The man dropped his cigarette.

'What kind of accident?' said the man.

'I just need to use your phone,' I snapped.

The man sniffed, fidgeted on his feet and then pointed back through the gate. 'Better come this way.'

Edging forward, I held up my hands in a don't shoot kind of way. 'I-I'm going to get help,' I said.

The Slap's eyes trailed my tiptoe steps – he lunged. I stumbled against the wall, flinching as his breath warmed my face. His gaze seemed impotent, he looked back to Chas, hand clenching, then back to me, back to Chas – all suggesting fizzled connections inside his meat head.

'There's a phone in the house,' said the man, his voice sounding forced and somewhat reluctant.

I shuffled my feet, building courage for a sidestep. The Slap appeared to have seized. Slyly, I moved across the wall, the man dressed in overalls drew closer. I took a long breath, glancing back at The Slap.

And then I ran away.

Back on the street I moved faster than I thought I was capable. My legs switched to cruise control and continued unawares as I gasped for breath and battled lactic acid. Six streets passed and my body seemed to double in weight. I struggled forward, as if a giant elastic band was pulling me back, but I could carry myself no longer. I hailed the assistance of a number thirty-eight. All I had was some loose shrapnel, but it turned out enough for a ride. I sat on the back seat, alone and trembling. My head was mush, I couldn't comprehend the shit I'd stirred. I had no clue what to do or even where I was going, but as home soon became the distance, one thing was glaringly clear – I couldn't go back.

Six

*I'll be your
best friend.*

Sleeping rough. Or rough sleeping. That night, either way described
my range of affordable accommodation. I mooched around the
city centre. My T-shirt and jeans were feeble protection against
a choppy November breeze and I cuddled myself. Darkness had
crept up. Music boomed from every pub like a pneumatic drill,
and as the theme bars flashed arrogantly, so they filled with kids
out of their heads on cheap booze. The city centre seemed much
more sinister post eight o'clock, scallywags and pushers lurking in
shop doorways, emerging from the crannies of the gaudy bars and
mucky pubs – I reckoned cosmopolitanism had been delayed at
Manchester since 1996. My pace became urgent. I stopped before
exhaustion, and after someone called me a ginger tosser – a back
alley and a cardboard box my bed for the night. The ring remained
within the depths of my pocket, such a little thing weighing so
heavily. The simple solution was to give it back, I knew that, just
not how. I could hardly drop by on Chas: 'All right mate, here's the
ring you were going to kill me for. By the way, how's that bump on

your head?' No, it had to be delivered – and by someone I could trust.

My sister was like me – she hated home. We talked sometimes. Sometimes we laughed. Her way was to be somewhere else and let boys fiddle with her.

But she was OK.

Morning arrived with all the cheeriness of living in a cardboard box beneath a grey sky. My musing had congealed into something you might call a plan, guiding me to a telephone box. In Hull, such oldie telephone boxes were a cream colour – the only place in England to rebel against the ubiquitous red. I dropped a scavenged twenty-pence into the slot, my dialling evoking a cringe as I felt a peculiar moistness to the buttons. Outside, I watched a gaunt man step out from Jackson's supermarket and open a can of super strength lager. Inside, smelt of piss.

Ring ring.

Ring ring.

She has to be home, it's her giro day.

Ring-bloody-ring.

Pick the phone up you lazy bastards.

Ring...

''ello?' said a voice.

Eh? A man? That's not Dad...

''ello?'

'Is Mary there?' I mumbled.

'Eh?'

'Mary.'

'Naa.'

'Well, er, when is she back?'

'Dunno.'

There was a pause.

'Who is it?' said the voice.

'A friend.'

'Which friend?'

'Er...'

'Is that Ginger?'

What? Shit!

'It is innit?' said the voice.

'No.'

'Shit! Y're in some shit mate!'

'How—'

'It's Syd mate.'

Syd? Hang on a minute. 'What *you* doing there?'

'Started goin' out with yer Mary.'

'Where is she?'

'Out.'

'Where?'

'Dunno.'

'Where's Dad?'

'Watchin' telly with yer old lady. I've just brought 'em some cheap baccy. Wanna speak to 'em?'

'No!'

'Calm down Charlie Brown.'

'Look. When did Mary say she'd be back?'

'Dunno mate. Tell y'what though, Chas is after yer blood.'

I took a nervous breath. 'You must have an idea where she is?'

'Naa. Probably shoppin'.'

Fuck... I can't wait for Mary to decide on shoes or hair colour or tampons. 'Listen, I need you to do something for me,' I said.

'What?'

'Come and meet me.'

'What? Where?'

'I'll tell you in a minute; but first I want you to go in my room...'

'Yer room?'

'Just listen!'

He was quiet.

'Go in my room, and between my mattresses there's a magazine with something in it.'

'What?'

'My passport – it's with my jobseekers' book – I use it for ID.'

'No I mean what mag?'

'*Big Ones Monthly!*' I snapped, echoing around the phone box. He chortled. 'OK mate.'

'And Syd…'

'What?'

'Say it's double glazing on the phone.'

'Whatever y'say mate.'

I waited, smiling nervously to a man waiting outside.

Finally, after much fidgeting, Syd returned.

'Got it.' I could almost hear him grinning.

'I need you to bring it to me.'

'The porno?'

'*My passport.*'

'It'll 'ave to be this afters – I'm busy at the mo.'

'Meet me at the train station, in half an hour.'

'Are y'avin' a laugh? I've got things need doin'.'

'And I need you to lend me two-hundred quid.'

'What!'

'Please?'

It was quiet for a moment. And another moment. 'Y'll owe me a biggy!' he said.

'Thanks. And Syd?'

'What?'

'Not a word to anyone – and I mean *anyone*.'

'No probs mate.'

'Thanks… mate.'

With that our conversation concluded.

Outside, the man leered at me. '*Big Ones Monthly?*'

I blushed and trotted off. 'It's a fishing magazine.'

Seven

What d'you say?
Take my hand.

Amongst the bustle of Paragon Railway Station, I propped myself beside WHSmith – preoccupied with conspicuous attempts to look inconspicuous. Bodies spilled onto the concourse in flurries, having alighted from such exotic extremities as Selby. I felt myself fidget. Glancing up, massive iron arches supported a glass roof that appeared as fragile as my mental state. Syd was late. I expected he would be because he was an idiot – but it still unnerved me. So long as the ring weighed my pocket I'd be a wreck, and I yearned the relief of passing on its burden.

And then? I was only more determined to get away.

'All right Ginger?' A passport waggled in my face. 'What's up?'

There he was, my skinny speccy saviour.

'You're late,' I said.

'Bleedin' buses innit.'

'Anyone know you're here?'

'Chill out. Nobody knows nowt.'

He handed over my passport – I snatched it.

'Y'll need that – Chas ever finds ye 'e'll kill ye.'

No shit.

'Got yer cash too.'

'How much?'

'Next week's bloody wages!' He pulled an envelope from his inside pocket.

'Not here,' I said.

I peeped around before leading him across the concourse. We passed the fancy doors of the Station Hotel, my glance inside reciprocated by some prim looking old woman – I didn't know her, yet somehow she made me feel like a naughty schoolchild. I quickened my pace. Out into the car park, behind a hole in the fence, we settled on the sidings beside the disused platforms.

'I shagged Becky Smith round these parts,' said Syd, 'bent 'er over them buffers.'

'The money?'

He handed me the envelope nonchalantly. 'When's this comin' back. I'm no charity.'

'When I can. I promise.'

He gave a tut. 'The last promise I got round 'ere cost me one a them paternity tests.'

'Listen,' I said, 'I need you to do something else.'

'What?'

'About the ring.'

'What's the score? Y'floggin' it?'

'When you see Chas…' I dug it from my pocket, holing it out on an open hand. 'Give him a present.'

Syd stepped back. 'No way.'

'What?'

'Not like this.'

I stared at him.

'I mean… 'e'd flip if 'e thought I was in on it.'

'Just tell him it was a mistake.'

'No.'

I forced the ring onto him. 'Say you kicked my head in to get it – say anything – just make sure he gets it.'

His face seemed to pull in different directions. 'Y'can't just give it back – 'e wants to see ye… y've gotta get what's comin.'

'Eh?'

'Not like this.' He flicked his hand away and the ring jangled across the tracks. 'Make me fight y'for it.'

'What's the matter with you?'

'Pick it up.'

'Eh?' I pulled a face.

'Pick it up!'

I bent down, not because of Syd, but because I could imagine, painfully, what Chas would do if I lost the ring.

Syd kicked me in the face.

I fell.

'D-don't move,' he mumbled.

I held my head, blood trickling through my fingers. My senses were mudded, the world all at once distanced, as though my head were under water. The pain was acute and wholly disorientating.

Syd pulled me from the track, propping me against the buffers, his voice tremulous. 'Soz Ginger, I am.'

Pain restricted my communication to a dull grunt. I gazed up at him, my eyes re-focusing continually.

Turning away, Syd took out his mobile. 'It's me… Yeh. Behind the station… Naa. No trouble… Where? Couple a minutes?… Yeh. See ye.'

Still, I couldn't beat the pain to speak.

I watched Syd light a fag. He inhaled deeply, flicking the ash, and as he glanced back, for a moment our eyes held. He picked up the ring and it glimmered on his palm. It seemed to command his attention, as though it held the meaning of life. The moment lasted, long enough to whistle a decent tune, and then, finally, he looked at me and said: 'Mate, I've got loyalties.'

I'd have called him a bastard, but the pain just allowed me to groan.

'I dint wanna 'urt ye, honest.'

Honest? Ha – fucking – ha.

'Still mates though? I mean, this is just business.'

I blinked away a droplet.

'Yeh, just business,' he said decidedly.

I closed my eyes and drifted. Syd kept talking but my head throbbed louder. I was hurting, but I could take it – as he said, it was just business.

The world inside my mind was peaceful. Reality was distant and I could be anything, anywhere I wanted. I could be happy.

But there were voices, at first just whispers, but they amplified, to shouts, to bellows, and soon my sunny-seaside-ice-cream-van delusions became intolerable. They'd come to drag me back.

'What have you done to him?'

'I only kicked him in 'is 'ed.'

'How many times?'

'Dunno. Twice?'

'Dickhead.'

'I thought it's what y'wanted?'

'This was *my* pleasure.'

'Soz.'

'He's totally gone.'

'Naa.'

'And there's too much blood. I've taught you to be tidy.'

'It's 'is 'ed innit – yer 'ed always bleeds buckets.'

'Can he hear us?'

'Dunno. Maybe.'

My face was slapped, hard. 'Can you hear me?'

I groaned – the voice went through me like a fingernail running down a blackboard.

'You with it?'

I opened my eyes to Chas's fat face, its redness making me squint.
'Good.'

He punched me.

I screamed.

'That's better.' He moved up close, giving a sample of his less
than hygienic breath. A lump on his forehead stuck out like a small
plumb, I reckoned a memento from our last encounter. 'Now, listen
to me. I've got my ring, so I'm pacified.'

Funny, my throbbing nose doesn't quite see it like that.

'I can see you've had a kicking, so maybe I'll take that as even.
Understand?'

I groaned.

'I know you're not a daft lad, so I know you're not gonna say
anything. Right? No grudges, and no pigs.'

Groan.

'Good lad.'

I slumped a little further. Chas dug his hands beneath my pits
and sat me up. He peered at me, kind of curiously. 'You know, you've
got bollocks.'

Yes, I often play with them.

'More than your old man, that's for certain. You remind me of
me when I was your age – nobody going nowhere, waiting for your
chance to show 'em.' He moved closer still, his tone alluding less to
physical harm. 'I know what it's like to be a loser, you've gotta find
those bollocks and go for it. You have, and some. Trouble is you
fucked with the wrong fella.'

*I really didn't want to fuck, it just kind of happened, and then…
well, I was fucked.*

'You see, you've gotta have that bit extra, something upstairs.
Example: Syd over there – he's eager, maybe he's got bollocks – but
he's daft. I say, *he* does. He's a puppet.'

'What?' said Syd.

'Fuck off.'

'But...'

Chas glowered.

Syd trotted off.

'As I said – he's a puppet. But that's only entertaining for so long. I need someone who shows a bit of noddle – someone who can shift a mobile phone and know not to knock at the house it was lifted from. I've been thinking, maybe *you've* got more than the usual dickheads round here.'

I gave an empty stare.

'What do you say? Work for me?'

A job?

'Hundred a week – keep signing and you'll clear another fifty.'

With real money?

His face moved so close I could feel his breath on my eyeballs. 'I'm giving you a chance to be somebody, rise above the losers and earn respect. Your whole family's a joke – dad: sloven, mum: crone, sister: trollop. *You* can be different. Come on, what do you say?'

It was quiet, his breathing was heavy. The sight, the smell and the viciousness of his words: I was wholly repulsed. I drew what little energy I could muster. His horrible, fat face was grinning – I could bear no more.

I spat blood at him.

Chas didn't move. Time seemed to freeze but for the spit trickling down his face, its red trail like war paint. He rose to his feet, smeared his face with a calm brush of his sleeve, staring, not a twitch betraying the thoughts in his head. Then, from the depths of his bowels came a bellowing laugh – it was excruciating: 'Your funeral our kid.'

As he stepped away, a shadow came down, vast and dark enough to render a chill. I saw The Slap. He was towering, silent, ready at the snap of a finger.

And so that finger snapped.

The 2:15 arriving from Bridlington hid my cries from the world.

PART TWO

September 1999

Eight

*Coffee, tea and misery is an
exquisite brand of company.*

I gazed over a corrugated roof, the vents like tin mushrooms, regimented and poised to attack. They divulged the workings of the factory below via an unambiguous pong to any nostril within a half mile.

Fish.

My desk stood by a first floor window, within such proximity that sometimes I could taste the air. Still, at least I worked in the *office* above the fish factory – and the only fish I had to negotiate was a haddock in a top hat smiling back from the headed letter paper.

I sighed and dropped my tuna mayo sandwich into the bin – the last thing I wanted was fish for my bloody lunch.

'Not eating, Ginger?' said Brian, appearing next to me.

I didn't reply, his stealthy movement across the office rather off-putting.

'Everyone should have three meals a day, we owe it to ourselves. Our body is our temple.'

'Not hungry,' I mumbled.

My stomach growled in disagreement.

He prodded me. 'Sounds like someone's telling fibs. Have some of my couscous, I made it fresh this morning.'

'No.' I frowned so hard it felt like my forehead being cut in two. Brian reminded me of a ferret – he was always *there*, sniffing around. I often thought he'd run up my trouser leg given half a chance.

He sat back at his desk. 'So what's the particular reason for your mood today?'

'Piss off.'

Brian gave a tut. 'Charming! Sounds to me like you need to release some pent up frustration.'

'I'm fine. Thank you.'

'What about Donna on packing row two? She's hot for you.'

'She smells.'

'An occupational hazard Ginger. You don't smell too sweet yourself.'

'I hate fish.'

Brian shook his head. 'All you ever do is come to work and mope, then go back to that grotty bedsit, and mope.'

'But it's *my* bedsit, *my* rules, *my* life.' I looked away. 'And by the way, I don't mope, I'm a deep thinker.'

'You're a God-awful misery. Come to line dancing – we'd have a ball.'

'Prancing about to *Cotton-Eye-Joe*? Not my scene.'

'Well, feel free to wallow.'

I did feel free, and wallowed in the prospect of the coming afternoon lingering in a 'can't be bothered to work' kind of a way. I mean, a paper willy can only entertain for so long – and I didn't know how to make a pair of tits. I was startled from such considerations by a visitor:

'Good afternoon gentlemen. Working hard? Good, good!'

Brian stood to attention. 'Hello sir. How are you?'

'Fine Bri, just fine. Ginger?'

I grunted.

'That's great.'

This recently arrived person was Mr Fish – he may have had a proper name, but I didn't much care.

He grinned, flashing a gold tooth. 'Keeping my factory in good shape?'

'Of course, sir,' said Brian.

'Good, good. Well gentlemen, today, I've brought my daughter along.'

The bloated rich bastard stepped aside, tucking his thumbs beneath his braces. Beside him, I noticed a disgustingly primped girl, made up in a flaunting frock like a cover of *Cosmopolitan* magazine. She was pretty enough to make me stare and reserve a mental snapshot for moments alone. As she acknowledged us with a short flare of her nostrils, I named her Ms Fish.

'I'm giving a tour of the factory – the ins and outs of how everything works.' Mr Fish looked to his daughter and offered a soppy smile. 'After all sweetheart, it will all be yours one day.'

She appeared to squirm, and stepped away from a fatherly embrace.

'Right, well then,' said Mr Fish, clearing his throat. 'We've seen all the way from bread-crumb bucket to finished fish finger – here the journey ends.' He opened his arms to Brian and I. '*This* is the control centre, the brain behind the whole operation. Tell her what you do gentlemen.'

It was quiet.

Hmm. What do I do?

Still quiet.

Let me think…

'OK,' said Mr Fish, glancing to his watch. 'The way to go is to leave the three of you alone – what better way to explain than to see you in action?'

Brian's nose twitched. 'Well, sir, I'm not sure—'

"bout time I blew away the cobwebs in my office. I'll give you half an hour.'

Mr Fish gave a decided nod, smiling to his daughter and swinging his arms as he left the room. Ms Fish flared her nostrils and tossed a glance over the office, her blue eyes so beautifully condescending.

'Get me a coffee,' she said flatly.

Brian pulled a face. 'Sorry?'

'You heard me.'

'Manners cost nothing.'

She flicked her hair behind her shoulder – it was blonde, but not naturally – locking eyeballs with Brian. 'Stop slopping about, get your hands out of your pockets and make me a fucking coffee. *Please.*'

'Pardon me!' said Brian, indignant to the point of speaking like a girl. 'But we couldn't possibly spare the time. We have important work to do.'

'Like I said – slopping about, hands in pockets fiddling with your testicles. You hardly need to give me a demonstration.'

A sudden itch ensured she got one anyway. 'What's *your* problem?' I said, frowning.

'It speaks! Woken up have we?' As I offered two fingers, she laughed like a moustached supervillain. 'All it takes is one word from me and you're both out of here. I'd show a little more respect.'

'People earn respect,' said Brian, his arms flapping.

'No. It's inherent. Now, I want a coffee.'

I glanced at Brian, our reply was unanimous. '*Piss off.*'

Ms Fish returned a false smile, taking a moment to moisten her lips, before wailing: '*Daaaaddy!*'

Stumpy legs carried Mr Fish through in a sweat. 'What? What's happened?'

'They won't make me a coffee,' she mumbled, cuddling herself.

'What?' He gestured to us petulantly. 'Make her a bloody coffee.'

'Fresh out of coffee sir, that's all,' said Brian.

'I see a jar there.'

Brian gave a tut and shoved me. 'I told you.'

'*I* never said we'd ran out.'

'Gentlemen, I expect better!' Mr Fish observed us, several short sniffs suggesting a process of deliberation. After a while, his voice dropped and he spoke rather sternly: 'The accountant needs this month's time-sheets to be signed and sealed by the end of play today.'

'Again? We had to stay late twice last month,' said Brian.

'A couple of extra hours – you can have time and a half.'

'But—'

'Problem, Bri?'

'No, sir.'

'That's what I thought.' Daddy Fish and daughter Fish turned, almost in unison, and left the office.

Brian appeared close to spitting. 'Bitch. I bet she's a Scorpio.'

I shrugged, flopped back in my seat and fiddled with my testicles.

Nine

If only the world would
stop and take a hike.

The day had been long, and there was yet longer to go. I was tired, tired of every-bloody-thing.

'How you doing, chuck?' said Brian, packing up his desk.

I flicked a pile of time-sheets and they fell onto the floor.

'We're only getting paid until seven you know? You'll be here all night at that rate.'

I shrugged. 'I need a holiday. I reckon I should have flogged that ring and buggered off some place hot.'

'Like I haven't heard that a million times before. You need to make some changes Ginger.'

'A job's a job.'

'I don't mean that.' He waved his arms earnestly. 'You're nineteen years old – you can do whatever you want! Strive for new experiences, set yourself goals.'

'I did, I'm here and it's shit.'

'You can't set up base in one place, sit on your arse and expect to be happily-ever-after. Life's a learning curve. Look.' He tossed me a magazine. 'Suzi Star says Cancer will have an adventure this week.'

'What the hell do you know?'

'I know I'm happier than *you*.'

I pulled a face.

Brian gave a resigned sigh and stood up. 'Well that's me done... You don't fancy giving me a lift on that scooter of yours? Line dancing starts at seven – I'll never get to The Lion in ten minutes. Buy you a pint?'

I stuck up two fingers.

'Suit yourself. See you tomorrow then, misery guts.'

I ignored him.

Alone, I rocked back in my chair and allowed my muscles to unwind. The room reflected in the darkness of the window and I saw myself – a clean white shirt and fucking ginger hair.

I sighed.

A year ago, life had been Kilroy and avoiding puke on the jobcentre steps. I'd lodged in a flea pit with strangers called Mum and Dad – and I was so spotty.

Much had happened. Now, thanks to Tony Blair's New Deal, I was oh so self-sufficient – and I had OXY 10 cream.

I was alone.

A second reflection appeared. 'Still here Ginger?'

I didn't bother to look around, the only other person stupid enough to be there so late was the old-git security bloke. 'I reckon it'll be another late one,' I said.

'Overtime?'

'Yeh. Not that I get a choice.'

'Don't miss *Eurotrash* – a good bit of flesh on show tonight. I'm taping it.'

I grunted, looking around as he hobbled away. I didn't know why he had a limp – I didn't know who he was really.

So, me and the time-sheets.

I laid my head on the desk, resting my eyes for a moment. Video Extra had a free kebab offer with every rental, and I thought any ⊠ *contains strong sex* would do nicely to see me off to sleep that night. *Anything* to help me sleep would be better than lying awake with thoughts of days, events, people gone by...

I dropped from the edge of slumber and said hello again to reality. My senses warmed and I wiped drool from my chin – my watch showing half eleven and a four hour zonk-out. I heard movement, not far away, pussy footsteps, scurrying. The sound seemed too nifty for the old-git security bloke, and as such, curiosity ventured me out into the corridor. I'd heard a rumour of the security bloke stripping off and wriggling about in the boss's leather chair – such a mental image induced a shudder as I followed the carpet to Mr Fish's office. I found the door ajar, the room behind presenting itself with the tastelessness of someone with too much money – wood panelling, bizarre porcelain shapes and a naked security bloke. He sat still, eyes closed with a contented grin, his skin sagging, so leathery and old.

'Ugh, cover up!' I shouted, prodding him with a gold pen.

The chair swivelled, and as his face moved away, so the leathered back came around. I could smell TCP.

And I could see blood.

His bald spot showed a gash that was jagged, vital fluid drizzled over the back of the chair, a pool upon the carpet. I hid beneath my hands, screwed up my eyes.

Deep breaths – in through the nose, out through the mouth.

I peeked through my hands.

Bugger, he's still there.

'Get a grip Ginger, get a grip,' I repeated, and again. I took a longer look. He was breathing, maybe. 'Ambulance!'

Across the desk, I dialled a phone in the shape of a dollar symbol. 'Ambulance... And police! I'm at—'

The line went dead.

The old git looked dead.

And someone was pointing a gun in my face.

'You shouldn't be here,' said a voice, muffled.

'T-time-sheets,' I stuttered.

'It's late?'

'I-it's my job.' I could see only gun, and as the weapon pressed into my forehead, I thanked God for my stellar anal tone. 'W-what do you want?'

'Close your eyes.' The voice was deep, sounding forced – a disguise.

I did as I was told, quickly and without a peep.

'Turn around.' The gun dug into the base of my head. 'OK. Open your eyes... Walk this way, to the painting.' It was of a fish. 'Take it down.'

A safe?

'Key in the numbers I tell you.'

I was dictated a number of digits, which I prodded into a keypad.

'Open the safe...'

That's a lot of money!

'Good.'

A leather bag was dropped beside me.

'Fill it.'

I scooped out thousands and thousands of pounds, my hands like piss in the wind.

'Zip it.' The gun was eased from my head. 'Put your hands up against the wall... *Don't* turn around.'

The fear in my hands gave a salsa beat as they wrapped on the wall panelling.

'Now don't move.'

I didn't.

It fell quiet, I could hear blood drip. The salsa slowed, *thank you ladies and gentlemen, and now the waltz,* echoing into a trickle.

And so it stayed, for what seemed like a fortnight.

Drip.

Drip, drip.

I glanced to a side. The security bloke was still leaking. So much red, thickening pools draining his existence.

I could be killed!

I shuddered.

Oh why me? Can't we just talk about this?

I took a deep breath, took a hold of my quivering and turned around.

No-one.

The relief was brief – *Woo-hoo!*

I stumbled out into the corridor, down the iron steps, across the factory floor. Out through the loading bay, I found my Lambretta rusting in the dark. A frantic kick-start proved impotent. Sirens sounded far away, moving in. Again, I tried the kick-start – the engine spluttered, died – as an old friend arrived to thwart my escape.

The gun.

If the gun had been a girl, I'd have reckoned it fancied me. It wasn't, so I guessed it was trying to kill me. Darkness concealed the figure attached – though I could imagine a grimace of the 'I'm going to fucking kill you' variety.

Sirens were no more than a street away. The scene was still, as though the pause button had been pressed. My heart pounded like it was trying to escape, my whole body moist. The gun lowered a little, the figure stepped forward. I strained to see what had been revealed from the shadows. Sirens were almost upon us. A flash of headlights caught a moment that lingered in its brightness. Never before had my mouth dropped out of control. She was beautiful.

She was Ms Fish.

Ten

Daddy is rich,
rich on fish.

The lollipop lady outside my school always used to buy me a packet of Maltesers for my birthday – she was wonderful.

Then one day she was sent to jail for a hit and run.

As then, I had the same 'how can this be' feeling towards Ms Fish. She prodded me with her weapon, her black figure effortlessly superior. Our eyes held – they were so blue, I could have lived forever in those eyes.

'Make the scooter work. Now, you shit!'

I obeyed the gun, the engine firing on the first kick-start.

She pulled on a balaclava, swung the bag over her shoulder and climbed on behind me, digging the barrel into my kidney.

An ambulance, a police car, there all at once, so much light, sound, I felt drowned.

'Go!'

We took off across the car park like shit off the proverbial stick, onto the street, our buzz resonating along the looming bricks of industry.

'Where?' I screamed.

She jabbed the gun harder. We followed to wherever my quivering hands may have steered.

And the sirens came with us.

'They're behind. Go faster.' Her breath tingled in my ear.

I tightened my grip on the throttle. 'This *is* faster.'

Blue lights sparkled in my mirror, the accompanying holler reaching deep into my guts. Adrenaline was all I had, it held me like a puppet – static without control, but Ms Fish had her hand up my backside.

I cut up the kerb – the bump strangely pleasurable – onto the passage behind the old oil seed mill. My mirrors shattered and bent inwards, sparks galore as they grated the brick. It was a rough ride down to the riverside, Ms Fish easing the gun to hold on tight. Out at the far end, the water was calm, on the surface a shimmer of light mocking our movement. Such a clear night made it cold, and as I gripped the throttle, I saw my fingers were a girlie pink. We made ahead, negotiating the skeletons of riverside industry, and killing the stillness with our incessant buzz.

'Follow the river to Drypool Bridge,' said a voice in my ear.

'What?'

'Drypool Bridge!'

A stray oil drum obstructed our path, forcing me to stop of a sudden. Ms Fish jolted forward, bounced off my back and hit the ground.

I looked down, gripping the throttle to prevent my hand from shaking. 'You OK?' I mumbled.

She was a heap, but a very pretty heap. Her head appeared from somewhere between her legs, and through the clinging weave of her polo neck, I noticed two erect nipples.

Oh right, she's still got that gun.

She stood up, and pulling away her balaclava, her blonde hair spilled over her ears. 'You shit. I'll kill you.'

You can load those nipples and shoot me.

'Say something!'

I stared at her, so beautifully ruffled. 'G-ginger,' I mumbled.

'What?'

'People call me Ginger – not Shit.'

She pressed the gun into my forehead. 'Drypool Bridge – *Shit.* Now.'

Maybe I should stop looking at her tits...

'Look at my face!'

Yep.

She lowered the gun and struck me across the face – I couldn't help but vocalise the pain, my wail hung in the air like a fog horn. Her eyes opened wide and she pulled me from the scooter.

'I know what *you* want,' she said.

This all to end. A warm bath. A mug of Horlicks. Are you a mind reader, madam?

She moved in close, her breath warming my neck. 'Me. Don't deny it.'

'What?' I blurted.

'I *know*.' Her voice became deeper as she trailed a finger down from her belly button to God-knows-where. 'You want it.'

Yes, fair comment.

'The question is, what you going to do about it?'

But you're a fantasy, a bit of posh ready to compromise yourself when I can't be bothered to lift the mattress for a copy of Big Ones Monthly.

I gave an audible gulp, an erect nipple between us. We were still. I felt uncomfortable, like I wanted to whistle.

'Well?' she said.

'W-what do you want me to do?'

She pulled up her top lip arrogantly, almost like Elvis. 'Don't give me questions... give me cock.'

Such requests were infrequent enough for me to remain rooted to the spot.

Gently, she took my hand and placed it in-between her legs. She gasped. 'You must never tell – I'll deny everything...' Her voice dropped further and rode upon her heavy breath. 'Quickly.'

So I kissed her. Her arms closed around me and we drooled over one another, the gun hanging loosely behind my head. I fiddled and squeezed, like when the nozzle on the tomato sauce got blocked. Her gloved hands probed under my shirt. My skin tingled under the leather, goose bumps sprouting at her every touch. A wind picked up, wrapping us in her lovely long hair and making me retch as a strand tickled the back of my throat. She pulled away, and in the grope of a breast, we were hit by the most intense light. I was blinded by its purity – it was angelic. We grasped one another, the wind beat our faces, so strong we had to gasp for breath. My senses were overloaded, I thought it was my calling – though I could think of more convenient times.

And then, like an articulated lorry, came a voice:

'Police! Stop, hands behind your head, lay on the ground.'

Unless God was a helicopter, I'd been hideously mistaken.

Ms Fish untangled herself from me, 'The scooter. Go!' She enticed her helpless accessory by digging the gun into my kidney – I wished my erection would go away.

I kicked the scooter into action, swung around and we took off. The helicopter hovered above and we glowed in its spotlight. I battered the throttle, weaved a path through cranes and containers, yet the spotlight held us centre stage. I cut across Drypool Bridge, following the opposite bank into the old town.

'We can't outrun the police,' I shouted.

Ms Fish growled. 'Keep going.'

Sirens sounded in the near distance and I pulled back on the throttle. Humber Street headed through the early morning fruit market and out onto the marina. We passed Minerva Hotel, the old Pilot Office and completed a circle back to the riverside. There was nowhere to go – the end was closing in.

Our presence echoed and filled the streets, the spotlight as bright as day. Ahead, our destination appeared as a wall of corrugated iron, and our speed suggested this was urgently desirable. I eased the throttle, and Ms Fish pointed over my shoulder. There was a hole, perhaps big enough if we huddled.

Indeed.

Cautious steering found us over the riverbank, a cobbled path descending to the mud and water.

I paused.

'Down,' said Ms Fish.

'What?'

The gun was so persuasive.

I edged forward. The sirens were closer.

'Move.'

A tentative pace took us down over the cobbles, the scooter spluttering under my nervousness.

'This is suicide,' I yelped.

'All the way.'

We came to rest, water tickling the front tyre.

I took a deep, shaky breath. 'What now? I can't bloody swim.'

'Look.'

The spotlight swayed gently, splashing its light onto the riverbank.

'The sewer?' I said.

'The old smuggling network, the tunnels stretch miles under the city centre. No helicopter can follow in there. Now move.'

I obeyed, steering the scooter a little up the bank. The wheels spun in the mud, sliding from behind as though I'd filled it with vodka. Ms Fish grabbed me tight – I quite liked that. I made sure we slid about some more.

The hole was capped with a huge grate, the hatch having been forced. My battered scooter fitted comfortably into the putridness. The headlight penetrated deeply, showing a vast slime-lined subway – and my God how it reeked.

'I think I'm going to puke,' I said, gagging as the stench hit the back of my throat.

She pointed the gun onward. I obeyed, of course.

We sped through squelchy stuff, our echo giving the sound of a hundred scooters. The distant darkness enticed us to deeper darkness, intersections branching to the same but different. I imagined the people above, drinking, dancing, sleeping, making love, each oblivious to the felons beneath them – for that's what we were. Perhaps, deep in the city's intestine, we were safe now.

I crashed.

I hit something big and sufficiently solid to catapult us over the top and land us ten yards down the tunnel. The slime broke my fall wonderfully well – though did little for my sex appeal. Ms Fish screamed and cursed.

'You OK?' I said.

'I'm rolling about in shit!'

Indeed she was – it was strangely arousing.

The scooter was a tangle, the headlight pointing to more muck dripping above us.

Ms Fish scrambled to her feet. 'I should shoot *you* right now.' She pointed a dildo at me.

'Wonder how that got round the u-bend,' I gasped.

She shrieked, dropped it and began to sift through the shit.

If only Daddy could see you now.

'It's gone.' She screamed and kicked the scooter.

The headlight jarred, and like a heavenly beam, showed a small inlet, dripping.

'Enough!' said Ms Fish. She dragged her swag bag, stuffed it up the inlet and proceeded to crawl behind.

'What about me?'

'Exactly. What about you?'

I watched her bottom squeeze in, and like the Pied Piper, it called for me to follow. We fumbled and slipped in a vaguely upwards direction – I took full advantage of the bottom touching opportunities, racing to a tally of six.

'You stuck?' I said.

'I can hear people on the street.'

We fumbled some more.

'Help me lift the cover,' she said.

I wriggled up beside her, our bodies so close I could feel her heartbeat.

She looked disgusted with me. 'Lift.'

Our joint effort budged it only a couple of inches.

'Again?'

A bigger effort produced a loud grunt and slid the cover onto the street.

'After you,' I said.

She sniffed, tossed the cash up first and was quick to scramble after it. Her bottom brushed over my face – I followed.

Gasps and mumbles greeted us as we emerged outside LA's nightclub. A couple of spangly outfits received specks of slime, and a couple of boyfriends looked rather unimpressed – further indication for us to keep running.

I followed Ms Fish across the street, round the back of the taxi office.

'What now?'

'Now? Now you piss off.'

'What?'

'You've expired your usefulness.'

'But… the police.'

'Just deal with it.'

She glared at me. She was still beautiful, so very. With a gentle touch, I wiped the slime from her face.

'Don't even think about it.'

'I thought—'

'You thought wrong.' She tossed me a bundle of notes. 'For the rust bucket.'

'But—'

'But nothing.' She walked away.

I watched the darkness take her, a confidence to her step that only beautiful people have.

What a ride.

What a fantastic arse.

Eleven

Smiles are so outdated
and laughter's overrated.

My bedsit smelled.

I could never quite place it. The woman upstairs said a man had died in there once – perhaps the smell was suggesting they'd never found him. I don't know if all this had anything to do with the stain on the mattress.

Like a mole, I lived in a hole.

The early hours had given little cover for the way home, not with the conspicuousness of being drenched in slime. More than once, party people had delighted me with the pissed up wit of: 'You stink of shit.'

But I was home.

In the hall, the girl next door passed with a man on her arm – she gave most of her massages at night. Upstairs, the theme to *Kojak* echoed through the building – *that* bloody woman had her telly on 24/7.

But I was home.

I opened my door and blundered into the darkness. The electricity had been off for two days because I hadn't had fifty pence for the meter. I groped the wad I'd shoved down my pants and felt a pleasant tingle – the meter didn't take fifty-pound notes. Perhaps, for a second, I thought about the police – then I tried not to think. I lit a candle and reckoned on a bath. Anyway, I knew it wasn't my fault – she had a fucking gun, and who ever pointed a gun affectionately?

Oo, I remember, I've got some lovely bubble bath.

I dragged my weary self into the bathroom. The candle flickered in time to my stumble and we danced together, I felt almost elegant. I wanted to shout 'I'm alive', for I wasn't dead. But I was quiet. My hands were shaking and I spilled my bubble bath. 'Oh God,' I wailed, 'not the bubble bath!'

I slumped on the floor and cried.

Twelve

When we're close we're held
apart, either side of no affection.

I awoke in much the same place. The sun blasted through a sheet covering the window, creating the silhouette of a sick stain on the wall. My face warmed in such rays, the muck from the night before like a protein face-pack.

Life returned, then I remembered.

My guts churned inside me. I remembered the security bloke, I remembered Ms Fish and I remembered the money.

Fuck.

Nervousness took a hold like poison and I shivered. I dug the swag from my pants, my eyes darting around the bathroom as I grasped desperately for a thought of what to do.

Upon a tiny shelf by the sink, stored in a re-sealable sandwich bag, I kept my toothbrush. Apparently, every bathroom contains millions of microscopic faecal particles, just floating around in the air. That thought had always made me retch – hence the rather anal habit (pun unintended) of bagging my toothbrush.

I sacrificed my sanitation, exchanging my toothbrush for a wad of cash and pressing the sandwich bag so tight it made my fingers go white. My eyes then settled upon the toilet. I opened up the tank, tossed in the cash and slammed it shut.

Phew! Breathing space.

'Oi!' a voice cried out from behind me.

Startled, I hit my head on the sink.

There was heavy breathing, like a cement mixer. The sound elicited the fear of a perverted intruder, an imminent sexual assault. I grabbed the nearest makeshift weapon, scrabbled across the bathroom and out into the living room/master bedroom/kitchen. I pointed a loofah as threateningly as I could fake. Across the room, a skinny figure cast a shadow easily mistakable for a person made of celery sticks. A haze of cigarette smoke encircled me – Silk Cut. Childhood exposure had made such cigarettes a member of the family. Indeed, as the fog cleared, I noticed a familiar taint of coal tar soap to the air. Any fear of rape faded, and through strained eyes, I squinted towards the door and a person I once knew.

'Mum!'

She hollered. 'What you playing at? What's that smell? You stink.'

I spluttered as she blew a lung full of smoke into the room.

'Is that all you've got to say after all this time?'

I just looked at her.

'Well?'

Fine – I'm a fugitive, I'm an accessory to robbery and I'm so fucking scared I feel like my innards are putrefying. How's that? 'I've been busy,' I said.

'You've been selfish.'

I shrugged, though the action felt rather feeble. 'Work and stuff.'

'You could have been dead for all I knew.'

'I'm not.'

She grumbled through her fag. 'Sometimes I shudder to think what I've brought up.'

Fuck, I don't need this. I don't need you. I dropped the loofah, my frame slumping. Mum reminded me of a bad taste, the type that comes back every time you belch. 'What you doing here?' I said. 'The council fumigating fleas again? Bet Dad'll be happy.'

Her fag trembled upon her lip, dropping ash onto the floor. 'I've left Dad at home – *you* might try locking your bloody front door.'

'It'll take more than fumigation to get rid of *him*.'

Mum sniffed. 'Not my problem.'

'He should get his fat arse out of that chair – at least make the little buggers work for his blood.'

She snapped. 'There's no fleas.'

You know what? I don't even care. If you had any clue of what happened to me last night... I looked at her – she was like a mop, short with greying, greasy hair that straggled behind her ears. *Actually, even if you did know, you'd still be mean and emotionally debilitated. You haven't got a fucking clue.* I frowned. 'What you doing here then?'

'I've left him.'

'What?'

'I've *left* him.'

My mouth dropped, literally.

'It's over.' She sliced the air. 'End of story.'

I was simply stunned. 'What? You've put up with him for twenty years – a few more won't make much difference.'

'Things have changed. I've grown.'

I almost choked. 'Hang on a minute, just slow down.'

'Your father's ignorant. I don't wanna be part of his life.'

Astonishment took my voice to another level. 'But... who'll do stuff for him? *I'm* not.'

She gave a sarcastic snort. 'He's no more disabled than me. When Social find out the truth he's had it.'

'But you're both mean and miserable. You go together.'

'Maybe I've realised things can change.'

Mum's life was habitual, her marriage was habitual – change came only from the TV remote. 'So... you've met someone?' I said.

She inhaled deeply, dropped her fag and gazed at the cobwebs on the ceiling. 'I told you, I've just grown as a person.'

I'd have thought it was a wind up, but Mum didn't have a sense of humour.

She rubbed her sleeves, looking awkward, her grubby cardigan clinging to the skin and bone. 'I've thought about Islam,' she said.

I stared at her.

'Been thinking a while now.'

My power of speech seemed to be lost.

'You know what I mean? Muslims and that?'

Yes, I know what the words mean – what confuses me is the open mouth from whence they came.

'Like Nelson Mandela.'

My verbal backlog cleared a little: 'Nelson-bloody-Mandela! What the hell are you on about?'

'Like I said.'

'But he's not...'

'What?'

'Bloody hell! *You?* Religion? God?

'Why not?'

'You can't just *be* a Muslim. You need to... I mean...' I was bloody flummoxed. 'You just can't.'

'No law against it.'

'What is this? Hormones, or you been at the gin?'

There was something in her voice, it was unusual, kind of warm. 'It was the Arab woman who brings the Betterware catalogue,' she said. 'I found a copy of the Qur'an in my Shredded Wheat tidy.'

'Sounds like veggie meat.'

'Show respect!' She inflated her chest.

I pulled a face back in return. *Mum's only ever this passionate when Tom Selleck's on telly – my God, she's serious!*

Mum gazed, at nothing in particular, almost wondrously. 'I admit, at first, I used it to prop up the wonky bed leg – but then football was on and Dad started shouting at the telly again. I went to bed for some peace – got bored – so I read the Qur'an.' She smiled, briefly. It was unnerving: I'd seen her smile once before – 1996 I think – when she won a sweep on how many horses would die in the Grand National.

'It takes you all week to get through *Woman's Own.*'

She glanced away. 'It was a short version, with 3D pictures.'

'A pop-up book?'

'It was meant for her nephew – *Quran Stories For Kids.* You pulled a tab to cover Mohammed's wife in a hijab.'

I turned away – it was the stupidest thing I'd ever heard. 'I haven't got time for this.'

'Listen! The point I'm making is *respect.*'

'Eh?'

'You haven't seen the Betterware woman, how her husband adores her – he treats her like a princess every day. Last week it was her birthday: he filled the house with her favourite flowers and scattered rose petals wherever she walked.'

'Did he clean up afterwards?' I said.

'That's not the frigging point! Do you know what I got on my birthday? Fish and chips. And *I* had to bring the bugger in from chip shop.'

'Well their type like to be over-the-top.'

'They respect their women. And it's about bloody time *I* was respected.'

'By pretending to be a Muslim?'

'I'm not! I'm making a point. I'm not some silly bint who can't control her hormones. I'm a woman. A *woman.* And I used to dance. *I* danced. And Dad danced with me. And it didn't matter that he had two left feet. And now I don't dance. I *don't* fucking dance! Because I fell in love. I used to be in love!'

I didn't know what to say, so I ignored her and made for the bathroom, but she came for me like one of those charity street hustlers. *Right – I need to shower, change and get to work... Work! Oh fuck! It's all such a mess. I mean, what the hell am I supposed to do? Just turn up? Mooch through the door like it's a regular mind-numbing-job-hating-fish-fragranced day?*

'I've *left* your father!'

You know, Mum, being a short, antagonistic distraction could well have been the nicest thing you've ever done for me. But now, like a thunderclap, it's all back in my head, and...

'You listening? I'm destitute.'

And you just seem so trivial.

'Go back to him Mum,' I mumbled.

'I can't. I just can't.' She paused, for what seemed like an hour. 'I need a place to stay.'

I didn't own a suitcase, though as I glanced by Mum, I noticed a 1970s trunk-like thing placed just inside the front door. 'Don't you dare think... No – no way.'

She grumbled.

'No.'

She was pained to say it: '*Please.*'

'No. It took me nineteen years to get away – you think you can just swan back in here.'

'I ditched the dancing for you, nineteen years that I cared for you – payback time sunshine.'

'Get lost.'

She slapped me.

I held my face. 'You bitch.'

'If I had any other choice I would get lost,' she screamed, 'far away from *you*.'

'So go.'

She thumped me, and again. 'Show me respect I'm your mother!'

I pushed her away and she fell over the bed like a withered hag. As she struggled to straighten herself, the sun caught her through the window and I saw a tear glimmer in her eye.

I was disturbed. 'You're crying,' I said.

She turned her head away.

'You're crying.'

Her sleeve wiped over her face.

'I didn't mean...'

She grabbed her suitcase and made for the door.

'Wait.'

She ignored me.

'Mum...' I grabbed her arm.

She glared.

I looked away. 'OK. You can stay – just for a while.'

It was quiet. Awkwardness embraced us. I could hear the blood in my veins, my guts squirm. Then, struggling as though it were her final breath, Mum said:

'Thank you.'

I left for work an hour later, having scrubbed myself viciously. Out on the street, my pace was tentative, as though I'd trapped a stone in my shoe. The tree lined Boulevard was made of terraced villas, built for Victorian trawler owners, though a century-long greasy pole had landed the houses in a state of decomposition, carved up by cheap plasterboard to squeeze in the extra benefit cheques. A car pulled in ahead of me, the wheels still turning as the door opened into my path. I stopped. A man with a brown moustache climbed out and stared at me. I stepped aside, but he stared, a shadow falling as a body stood behind me.

Shit. According to last week's chip paper, muggings have risen 10% in the past year. 'I've got nothing.' I trembled as I turned out my pockets. 'Look – nothing. I've got nothing.'

He stared. 'Mr Jones?'

I nodded. *Hang on, how…?*

He flashed me a badge. 'Inspector Briggs, this is my sergeant.' A tall man appeared from behind me. 'Can we offer you a lift?'

This rendered little relief. 'A lift?'

'Yes, *sir*.' The words accompanied a horrible sarcasm. 'Running a little late?'

My eyes opened wide. 'I over-slept. Thanks, but I need the fresh air.'

'Don't muck me about, sunbeam.'

'I'm not…'

He swung open the back of his car. 'Get in!'

I acquiesced.

Thirteen

I thought I had it sussed that
my life would just come good.

My short ride to the police station was uncomfortable and I huddled myself in the back. Beside me, the tall one turned intermittently and peered down what seemed like a thousand miles of spotty nose; while the other cursed at anyone for his own bad driving – it was as if both faces were attempting to manifest the word 'unamused'.

To the rear of Redbourne Street Police Station, we pulled across the car park under the gawps of coppers on a fag break. A vault-like door granted access, and as I glanced skyward for some ethereal direction, I saw a sandstone lintel carved with the date 1885 – I shuddered and couldn't help but imagine the figures as a prison sentence. Inside, I tried hard to restrain my trembling and was subdued to a downwards glance as the duty sergeant confirmed various details about myself and the circumstances surrounding my being there, before allowing the two policemen to escort me to an interview room.

'Sit down,' said the one with the moustache.

I obeyed, huddling into a plastic chair. Tash unbuttoned his suit jacket, letting a spare tyre sag over his belt, and gazed out of the window – sunlight caught his facial hair, a speckle of ginger bristles indicative of tobacco use.

'Now then sunbeam,' said Tash, observing me like I expected he did modern art – without affection. 'We need to ask you some questions. Got the gist?'

I nodded.

'You're not under arrest – we call this an informal chat. Right?' Tash gestured towards the table and a rather dated tape recorder. The plug was disconnected from the mains with cable strewn over the machine, somehow conspicuously. ''less you want legal advice that is, then we have to fill out forms, get a duty solicitor...'

Someone to stick up for me? So I don't have to? Sounds perfect. I fidgeted in my seat, as though preparing to pass wind. 'Well actually I think—'

'What?' Tash snapped.

'That I need...' His acute frown scrambled my thinking and the remainder of my sentence was lost.

The tall one sniffed, sat at a diagonal to me, his lanky limbs collapsed into the chair like a folding clothes horse.

'Saying you want a shyster? Eh?' said Tash.

Assuming he meant legal representation, I nodded, coyly.

He looked away in apparent disdain. From an inside pocket, he removed a *Nicorette* branded blister packet, chipolata-esc thumbs pressing at the gum much like an autistic kid with bubble wrap. He appeared to think hard, frown some more, and then return the gum to his pocket. 'Sergeant Johnson,' he said, addressing his colleague rather dourly. 'Mr Jones here says he wants a shyster. That means we must oblige.'

The two policemen exchanged a glance and some sort of facial twitch, before Tash sauntered across the room, hands in pockets, kicking his feet into the floor. Standing by the table, opposed to me, he plugged in the tape machine and smiled. 'You're under arrest on suspicion of aggravated robbery...'

My holding cell offered a toilet, a bed and four walls, all in rather claustrophobic proximity – pretty standard stuff I reckoned. After an hour alone, staring at the ceiling, a lumpy mattress aggravating my back, there was heightened sense of event when a second man entered the cell. In fact, incarceration had stretched out the laws of physics to a degree that said hour could only be measured after the event and with the benefit of hindsight.

So, this man beheld the cell with a curious expression – he looked old, post sixty, old enough to pass as my granddad. His gaze swiftly settled upon the occupant and seemed to recoil a little before he nodded to me in acknowledgement. He appeared scraggly, his beard a week too long, his suit bed-creased.

I stared. *Er... have you come to change the sheets mate?*

'Good morning dear boy!' he said. The words emanated from his decidedly suspicious beard, the contents of which suggested he'd had beans for breakfast. 'Mr Jones I trust?'

I nodded, kind of stunned, and pulled myself up to sit on the edge of the bed.

'Good to meet you dear boy, good to meet you.' There was a hobble to the couple of steps he took to shake my hand. His grasp was very firm. 'I've heard much about you. I'm not interrupting I hope?'

Interrupting what exactly? A spiral into self-harm? 'No.'

'Good. Coffee? Get the brain in gear.' There was a huff and a puff as he reached down for a paper cup I'd left on the floor.

'It's cold,' I said.

'Never mind. How about tea? Hmm?' He smiled, banged on the cell door and bellowed. 'Tea in here please. Two teas.'

And why not Jaffa Cakes?

'Now, dear boy, I expect you know why I'm here.' He hustled me along the bed and sat beside me.

I only hope you do, dear boy. I shrugged.

'Yes, well… first we should… sorry, er.' He thought for a second, then took some papers from an inside pocket and fiddled with them. 'Well, it would appear we have a pickle.'

'What?'

'Yes, quite a pickle.'

'You're him then?'

'Pardon?'

'The solicitor?'

'Sorry! How rude of me… John Edmund, of Edmund & Associates.'

Ok. That is a name. And it kind of sounds like it should. 'So you are?'

'Six years in the game – have no fear.'

Mail-order degree was it?

John Edmund rested a hand on my shoulder. 'I'm here to help, yes? You're not on your own.' He smiled, and I perceived it as genuine. 'Now, let me say one thing.'

I nodded.

'Guilty,' he said.

There was a pause. A baked bean fell from his beard and as it hit the floor quietness made it almost a thud. There had been no bias to his tone, just a bland matter-of-factness that seemed to suggest some kind of deal had already been done.

I shrugged his hand away. 'What?'

'I'm aware I could stir mixed feelings, yes? But trust me, dear boy, making an admission from the very beginning will reflect well in court.'

'But I'm innocent,' I blurted. *Well, not exactly, but I'm definitely not guilty.*

'Yes yes. Just consider, dear boy, that there's more than one way to cook an egg.'

'No way. I can't…'

Yes this is a pickle isn't it. Quite a fucking pickle.

'Of course, it's your prerogative,' said John Edmund. 'I merely advise you of the options.'

I gazed at the floor, unblinking until the grey concrete blurred my vision and then my thoughts. The options were trivial – a declaration of guilt, a declaration of innocence – neither could delay the blast-off of one fact:

I was fucked.

'Right then,' said Tash. 'What time you usually start work?'

'Half-eight,' I mumbled.

'Bit late today, eh?'

'Yeh.'

Back in the interview room, four poker faces hunched over the table – a stack of cash and a nebula of cigarette smoke away from an illegal gambling den. Tash sat opposed to me, intermittently massaging his right temple; the tall one sat at a diagonal, watching silently but for the odd deep breath, picking at the perfect-storm of acne afflicting his nose; and John Edmund sat beside me, doing not very much. All the while, a whirr sounded from the cassette recorder, almost like a meditation mantra.

'You've been conspicuous by your absence,' said Tash.

'Slept in,' I mumbled.

'Alarm clock bust?'

I shrugged.

'Heavy night?'

'Not really.'

I glanced to John Edmund, who gave a short nod, which was neither instructional nor reassuring. Indeed, before entering the interview room, there had been no consensus and no action plan. My shrugging and minimally syllabic replies were an ad-hoc remedy.

Tash sniffed. 'So, last night, where were you?'

'Work,' I mumbled.

'Time?'

'Late-ish.'

'How late?'

'Ten, eleven.'

'Notice anything unusual?'

'Not really.'

'That right?'

'Yeh.'

'Sure about that?

'Like?'

'Well, let's say…' Tash paused to rub his temple and perform an exaggerated eye roll. His gaze resettled over me, eyes widening and an aggressive tone to complement: 'A bloody armed robbery!'

I stayed quiet, tummy turmoil threatening the expulsion of bodily fluid.

Tash appeared yet more unfriendly: 'A man's been viciously assaulted, fifty-thousand pounds is missing. You admit you were at the scene – we have a witness who saw you give the robber a lift on your bloody scooter!' He leaned forward and pulled a face. 'I want some answers sunbeam, or you're in deep.'

He glared and I quivered.

'I'd advise no comment,' said John Edmund, a while later. His delayed response accompanied a smile that was rather peculiar and probably related to the daydream he'd awoken from.

My head slumped forwards and I offered little resistance as my face hit the table. *I just don't care. Leave me the hell alone!*

'Unless, that is,' John Edmund continued. 'Unless you'd *prefer* to comment?'

What? Does this bloke get paid in bananas?

I heard Tash readjusted himself, the chair seeming to groan under the weight of too many bacon butties. 'Well?' he said.

I hardly owe Ms Fish the loyalty of 'no comment', and this set of clowns can whistle for an explanation. Maybe I should be more concerned with which option gives me the least time in jail. Yes, quite a pickle.

I took a long, deep breath. 'OK,' I mumbled, sitting up.

Tash's eyes were wide and attentive. 'Ready?'

I nodded and cuddled myself. I wasn't cold, in fact I was clammy, but still I cuddled – it seemed to give a certain security.

'Right, in your own time,' said Tash.

So I braced myself, and talked. I was nervous, but I clung to a little composure – like when Stephanie Fletcher lifted her top behind the boiler room at school – I was brave. 'I fell asleep doing time-sheets,' I said. 'I woke up about half eleven. I heard something – I dunno what – so I looked around. I went into Mr Fish's office, and that's when I saw...'

He nodded for me to continue.

'Well...'

'Go on, you're all right.'

'I saw Willy Wonka.'

'What?'

I paused for breath, my heart pulsating, before adding: 'And an oompa-loompa.'

Fuck this set of jokers. I mean, either way I'm going to jail...

Tash appeared confused, an expression I reckoned similar to a demented grandma who'd forgotten that granddad was dead. 'Say again?'

'And then I saw the security bloke – he was bleeding. So I called for an ambulance, but the line was cut, and then—'

'Hold on sunbeam. You saw who?'

'The security bloke.'

'Before that!'

'Oh. Willy Wonka. He looked pretty cross – and the oompa-loompa had a gun.'

'So the robber was *dressed* as Willy Wonka?'

I shrugged. 'Maybe.'

Tash groaned, as though I'd delivered a terrible punch line, rubbed his temple and then frowned so hard I thought his face might turn inside-out. 'Don't do this sunbeam. Really, it aint clever.'

'But I can describe the gun?' I said, stumbling across the words impatiently.

He twitched.

'It was black and gun-shaped,' I said.

The room appeared decidedly unimpressed. Tash's eyes had latched onto me with an almost bloodthirsty fixation; the tall one mirrored the sentiment, I imagined as a kind of menstrual sympathy; and John Edmund had turned away slightly, body language communicating 'this cunt's not with me'.

'Are you for real?' said Tash.

'What?'

'Do you think I'm gonna sit here and take that?'

I shrugged.

'So,' he tapped his fingers upon the table, making a galloping sound – if it had been legal I think he would have wrapped said fingers around my neck, 'we're looking for Willy Wonka, an oompa-loompa and a gun-shaped gun?'

John Edmund stirred from his resignation: 'I'd advise no comment to that.'

I hesitated, considered, and then looked Tash directly in the eye. 'Yes,' I said.

The two policemen exchanged glances, an unspoken communication that seemed to make them both more agitated.

'I'll say this once. Right?' Tash snapped. 'Save us all a lot of trouble – tell the truth.'

I fidgeted. 'I don't know what else to say.'

'You acted as getaway driver – why?'

I shrugged.

'Where's the scooter now?'

My poor Lambretta, drowned in slime! 'Dead,' I said flatly.

'What d'you mean? What happened?'

I shrugged.

Tash took a deep, seemingly soothing breath. 'OK. So what happened to the gun?'

'I dunno.'

'The *money?*'

I shook my head. *I don't know much do I, Mr Policeman? I wish I did. Most of all I'd like to know the answer to actually giving a shit. And passion – you look like you wanna bite my nose off – where does that come from? How come I don't do anything unless it's under duress...*

'You said you had a witness?' I said, the words bursting from my mouth with an elevated tone. 'That saw me on the scooter?'

Tash nodded. 'That's what I said.'

'The witness saw the gun?'

A reply was not forthcoming, Tash sniffed and broke eye contact.

'So you know?' I said.

'We don't know anything 'less you tell us,' said the tall one, in what I reckoned a token contribution to get his voice on tape.

You know I was at gunpoint. You know I had no choice!

'I had to obey or I was dead meat,' I blurted. '*Dead meat.* He had a gun – no way was I going to argue against that. I did as I was told, I just wanted to live!'

Tash expelled his breath lazily, as though he anticipated a rigmarole and really couldn't be bothered. 'That right?'

'Yes!' *Well, there or thereabouts.*

'So what about Willy Wonka?'

Hmm, tricky. 'I got confused,' I said.

'Some people might call that delirium.'

'He was black,' I said. 'I mean, black clothes, a balaclava.'

'You need to give me more than that.'

'It's all I've got – a gun was in my face.'

'You're not helping me sunbeam.'

'I'm trying.'

'So why didn't you call us? Eh?'

'I'd have been dead meat – *dead meat*. He said I'd be hunted, and horrible things would happen – that's what he said. So, I was quiet.'

'Definitely "he"?'

I nodded. *Course, by that I mean 'she'...*

'Anything else?'

I shook my head. *A 'she' I almost fucked, by the way.*

'Think hard.'

I think if I don't tell, maybe I will fuck her... Or not lose my job. Either is fine.

'Something familiar? A voice? A mannerism?'

'Not really,' I said.

'Right,' said Tash, readjusting his girth. 'We're gonna go back, start again. Yeh? Pick through yesterday in detail – minute by minute.'

'I really don't think I'll remember—'

'OK?'

I glanced to John Edmund, who appeared to find more engagement from a greenish stain over his lapel. As such, I looked back to Tash and shrugged. 'OK.'

So that's what happened. Tash wanted to know everything about that day, questions came like artillery fire and everything from breakfast cereals to pooping habits were need to know. For the most part, I was happy to oblige – it's not like it mattered to me if he became privy to my preferred brand of bog roll. But, as we came to the meat and potato questions, I remained steadfast with my answers: I saw nothing, I knew nothing and I was shit scared. This gained me little sympathy, my stuttering and minimal eye contact, combined with an unwillingness to fess up, seemed to project a kind of false vulnerability that antagonised everyone. Though the perceived falseness was, in fact, false – it was just me.

After, roughly, the time it takes to change a duvet cover – ages – the questions stopped, as did the tape recorder, and Tash peered: 'You want some time to think?'

'No,' I said.

'You do realise we'll have to make further enquiries?'

I shrugged.

'In the meantime, you won't be allowed back to work.'

'What?'

'And you'll have to answer bail.'

I felt a tingle. *He's going to let me go?*

'So if there's anything else rattling around in your head – say it now.'

'Not really,' I mumbled.

Tash fished inside his jacket pocket, dropping a card and a packet of Nicorette gum onto the table – he passed me the card. 'If by some miracle you remember something, call me. Either way, we'll be seeing each other again.'

I sat and huddled into myself. *Dare I think I've fooled them? I'm not in jail, so that's good. But... maybe I should have told them the truth, I mean, what do I owe her? She's so—*

Tash pressed out a piece of Nicorette from its blister packet, the first chomp pretty vicious, and I reckoned on him wishing it to be my head. 'Stay out of trouble sunbeam, eh?'

In reply, I gave some kind of vague expression that didn't really mean anything, scared that if I made the wrong move I'd suddenly be the highest bidder on a night back in the cell.

'Duty sergeant'll sort out your bail,' said Tash, the two policemen then standing. 'Don't go booking any holidays.'

They both left the room without looking back.

It was very quiet, before John Edmund cleared his throat: 'Well, all said and done, I think that went quite well.'

Having wandered along the road, I settled my bum upon church steps a few hundred yards up from the police station. The

Church had been derelict years since, feelings toward Methodism presumably as cold as the steps made my cheeks. My slight tremor, however, did not stem from a chill, more the extraordinary events of the past twenty-four hours and my brain's attempts in processing them. The most recent were foremost and readily accessible: I had been told to answer bail every two weeks, reporting to Redbourne Street Police Station; and work had been declared a no-go zone, the precise conditions of which were lost amongst the haze inside my head. Simply, it was all a mind fuck.

'What have you told them?' said a voice, interrupting my cogitation.

I looked up. Ms Fish stood before me, parting the haze like Moses, but with better tits. Her smart, tight pencil skirt offered little room to manoeuvre as she took the four steps up to me, her pointy heels placed with firm self-assurance. As she leaned in, I felt her breath on my face. Her voice was soft: 'What have you told them?' She blew into my ear, it tingled, it was nice – before she bawled: 'Answer me!'

I jumped and spat out a knee-jerk reaction. 'Nothing, I've said nothing.'

She scowled.

'I mean… I told the truth, kind of. But not—'

'Fuck!'

'I haven't said… I mean… well… that it was *you*.'

'What was me? Nothing was me.'

I watched a bead of sweat trickle down her chest and disappear to a wondrous place.

'You saw nothing. OK?' she growled. 'Nothing. No faces. You keep to that story.'

I nodded to her chest.

'Got that?'

I nodded to her face.

Ms Fish stood up straight, collected herself, and perhaps was a little less heated. 'I'm glad we're on the same frequency.'

Again, her chest held my attention.

'And if you wondered…'

I looked up.

'I just like money.'

A moment's thought kept me quiet. *I don't think I'll ever like money as much as that…*

'What about work?' I blurted.

'Huh?'

'I can't go back – the police said. Not until…'

She smiled, certainly not sweetly, and brushed her fingers through my hair. 'I am sorry. But hey, maybe it's for the best.'

'I'll get paid?'

'What do you think I gave you last night? Lunch money?'

'No, but—'

'It's best for all concerned we keep our distance. I'll make sure Daddy gives you an adequate reference.'

'No way!'

'*Way*, there's nothing else to say.'

'Then I'll tell the truth – the *real* truth.'

'Like hell you will.'

'Nothing to stop me.'

'Cut the crap you bastard.'

We paused, staring at one another. The moment prolonged, extending into a face off, like opposing alley cats goading the first pounce. After a while, Ms Fish blinked, looked away and sniffed.

'Stay away from the factory and stay away from *me* – your wages will be paid as normal.'

I nodded, though she was already walking off. The clop of her heels faded into a backdrop of the city's hustle and bustle. Alone once more, a few minutes helped me un-tense and gradually I released some of the tension from my muscles, and a little wind. As I glanced around, the world seemed normal, and I felt, well, fine. I couldn't help but laugh out loud as the enormity, and indeed stupidity, of what had happened hit home. A confidence swelled inside me and for a moment I felt capable of anything.

Of course, it wouldn't last, and the reality of being me would soon shrivel that confidence to whence it came. But for the time being, I sat back upon the church steps, grinned and thought about Ms Fish's breasts.

I felt on top of the world.

Fourteen

Maybe if we spent some time,
we could understand each other.

'So how long do you expect to stay?' I said, curtly. The events of that day had buried Mum's lodging to the back of my mind. On my return home, her greeting evoked quite a frown. 'This is a bedsit for *one*, don't forget.'

'I've got cancer,' said Mum.

'What?'

'*And* AIDS.'

I yelped. 'You can't say things like that.'

She settled into the only chair, mother and furniture creaking in unison. 'Show a bit of kindness while you can.'

'You're *not* moving in – either go back to Dad or sort something else.'

'I'll live on the street.'

'Your choice.'

'I mean it.' She lit a fag, exaggerating as she inhaled. 'I don't know what's happened, I really don't. I can't think how it got to *this*.'

Well think harder. Think of a solution. Then piss off. I flopped on the bed.

'You see, there's givers and takers in life – and I've given *all my life*. Give. Give. Give. That's it.'

Really? It seems such gifts have gone, gone, gone.

'For what? Eh? You're all takers. Everything's changed! Dad can't see it. He can't think further than his next bloody meat pie. He won't listen.' Mum began to gesticulate with her fag. 'Back in the day we was a handsome couple.'

Back before colour TVs. And eyes.

'He was a smooth little bugger too – he used to balance a Mars Bar on his top lip, tell me to squint my eyes and imagine he was Tom Selleck. He was no Magnum PI, but he made me laugh. I think that's how I ended up with *you* in my belly.'

Oh here we go – another moan about 'the dancing'.

'Course, that's when I had to dump the dancing. I'll never forget, it broke my heart, I'd just been offered a second *Top of the Pops*. And *that* would've been the big one, the big break, I just know it – Lionel Richie was on that week.'

I sprawled out and looked at the ceiling. 'Whatever.'

She spluttered over her fag. 'Just you remember all I've done for you. I could've been on at The Palladium or Broadway. Who knows where dancing would've gotten me? But not *here*, that's for certain.'

'And now you're a Muslim?' I snapped.

'What?'

'Have you forgotten already?'

'No.'

'So how does that follow? I mean really, how does being a Muslim make up for not dancing?'

'I'm easing myself in, it's not definite yet.'

'It's not like buying a new settee, Mum.' I struggled up and frowned at her, I couldn't be bothered playing games. 'So what do you fancy for tea?'

She shrugged, puffed on her fag and aimed the smoke in my general direction.

'Go do that outside.'

'And catch my death? And what about rapists?'

'I need some fresh air.'

As Mum occupied herself with a copy of *Woman's Own*, I stood and made for the door.

Mum said after me: 'I fancy Chinese – but *you'll* have to pay.'

Out in the corridor, the woman next door was escorting a gentleman caller to her bedsit, Mum shouted something about egg fu yung and the man winked at me.

'Good time?' he said, I think translating Mum's food order into an act of deviancy/general age of recipient.

I shrugged. 'She's going free to any good home... Actually, *any* home.'

The women next door gave a tut and dragged his custom to her private parlour.

I stepped outside – it was all very clear really.

Mum had to go.

Fifteen

You're so obsessed with the world
around and how it's done you wrong.

Saturday – the day of dirty magazines and leisurely self-abuse. I'd
followed such an agenda for months, but now Mum had appeared
and the bathroom door didn't have a lock. So, *this* Saturday, I was
deviating from the norm.

As I alighted the number thirty-eight, a codger by the bus stop
grabbed my arm. 'Got a light, pal?' he said.

'No.'

'A quid for the bus?'

I kicked his cripple stick. 'Go fuck yourself.'

You see, I was feeling somewhat tense. Opposing, stood a block of
flats: a big, bland lump that tainted the landscape. Ten months respite
had changed very little – it was like an old photo of a bad haircut – and
having gone cold turkey, its exuding negativity caught me off-guard.
Memories intruded, refreshing past emotions. As such, I kept my head
down and quickened my stride, vowing my visit would be fleeting.

The door to flat 52 was a canvas of splatters and growths, each
having its own mucky history. In a past life, I'd opposed the door

many times, bracing myself – now you could hardly tell the door was green. Indeed, the bell was now nothing but a wire sticking from the door frame, and with little inclination for courtesy, I let myself in. There was no reply as I called out. In the living room, the telly mumbled amongst God knows how many dirty plates and dishes; and having exhausted the crockery, it looked like Dad had moved to eating meals from Mum's 70s vinyl collection. Voices drew my attention back into the hall. The stagnant air was stirred a little as my old bedroom spilled a conversation, closer steps making it coherent. Naturally, I earwigged.

'Just remember I'm looking after this baccy for a friend,' said Dad.

'I'm not bloody Customs.'

'Look, we have to get rid of it – *now*.'

'My mate'll be 'ere in ten minutes.'

'So will Social you tosser.'

I'd recognised the second voice immediately, a repulsion all-consuming and making me shudder. As I stepped into the doorway, I saw Dad rummaging through piles and piles of baccy, the duty on which could have fed and housed several DSS cases. Beside him, the second man looked up, the scene seeming to pause and force us to stare at one another. The months had held him in a time warp, he was the very same speccy weasel – the very same Syd.

'All right Ginger?' he said brightly. 'Long time no see.'

I didn't move – I just didn't know what to do.

Dad flinched and looked up, his fat face with the fear of a kid stealing his mum's ciggies. The fear turned to a frown as he recognised his son. 'What *you* doing here? Eh? Sneaking up on me! I'll batter you.' He raised his hand, and probably would have hit me if his sheer size hadn't reduced his movements to laboured wobbles.

Syd grinned, seemingly oblivious to his dishonour. ''ow y'been then mate? I 'ear y're workin' now? Fish factory innit?'

Was. And bail restrictions prohibit head-butting…

'*I'm* still workin' with Chas – I'm in on some big deals now – and I'm playin' with your Mary on me days off. I'm a man a multi-talents me. Yep, I'm on the up – and I'm gonna 'ave some big wonga to play with soon… Anyway, it's good to see y'fella.'

'Cunt.'

'Eh?'

'*Cunt.*'

''ang on mate, there's no need for nastiness—'

'After what *you* did?'

He sighed, as if to be spared a rigmarole. 'C'mon Ginger, that was yonks ago.'

'I spent three days in hospital.'

'Y'know it were just business – it never meant nowt about us bein' mates. I mean, y're *still* a mate.'

'You're a cunt.'

Syd shrugged. 'So y're Peter Perfect then?'

I was quiet. It was a necessity to think of myself better than *him*, he set such a low benchmark – simply washing my hands after taking a piss made me better. Yet I stood there, amidst an untriumphant return, effectively jobless and on bail for armed robbery. On paper that qualified me an even bigger cunt than the two opposed. I mean, I never thought *I* could be the one to rot in prison.

Dad piped up. 'As fascinating as this is girls – there's the small matter of all my baccy.' He grunted at me. 'And while you're here, you can help us shift it – make yourself useful.'

'I'm here about Mum,' I said, snapping onto his distraction.

There was a pause, then Dad looked away and burped.

'Well?'

He gave a grunt.

'You've got to ask her to come home.'

'Not a bloody chance!' he blurted.

'She's your wife. Does that mean nothing?'

'Don't mention her in this flat.'

'What?'

'Owt to do with her's barred.'

'What you on about? There's more of her here than *you*. Her silver jubilee stuff, her glam rock LPs, her fag burns on the settee – she's here whether you like it or not.'

'Only till I get a good price.'

'So you're happy doing your own dinner and tea? Bollocks.'

'She drove me bloody mad. She started doing all this weird and spicy food. We never had meat pie for a week – I'm not putting up with that.'

'But now she's driving *me* mad.'

'Not my problem.'

'But can't you see she's doing this for *you*? She wants you to notice her, respect her.'

Dad gestured at the baccy petulantly. 'If you're not gonna help, bugger off.'

Syd grabbed an armful. 'Dump it in the 'allway till Jim gets 'ere.'

I frowned. 'For God's sake, just talk to her.'

'Forget it,' said Dad. He plonked on the bed, sweating like the filthiest of pigs. 'It's over. We don't even speak the same language.'

'You never *did*.'

'I'm not sharing my bed with *that*.'

'But—'

'Full stop!'

I glared at him.

'Now help Syd shift that lot.'

'Help him yourself.' I picked up a bundle of baccy and drop-kicked it out into the hallway.

'Dickhead.'

I stomped out.

'Listen Ginger,' said Syd, stacking the baccy with the care of a dustman. 'I don't want no 'ard feelings or owt like that. So I was thinkin', I've got a bit a business comin' up. Thought y'might be interested?'

I looked at him.

'It's big. Only 'andful of us are in on it, Chas is bein' real careful. I can't say nowt else, but I reckon I can get y'in – Chas used to think y'were all right.'

'So you can double-cross me again? Got a couple of meatheads waiting outside for round two?' My voice dried, the final word but a whisper – I coughed away the bad memories.

'I mean it Ginger – this is *big*. I know y're still full of beef, but maybe this could be kind of a "mates" thing, like a clean slate. If I can trust ye?'

'Fucking trust!'

He glanced away. 'Well, if y'change yer mind – it's the marina Frid'y night, *Lady of the Humber,* 'alf eleven. But y'can't say nowt to nobody.'

A knock at the door interrupted my concentrated look of disgust, wild conjecture then making the imaginary meatheads seem plausible – I reckoned it time to escape.

Dad bawled from the bedroom. 'About bloody time – he's half an hour late. Tell your mate if he wants the full whack he can kiss my arse.'

Syd opened the door. 'Look Jim, I thought I said be 'ere for twelve…'

'Hello,' said a voice, 'David Owen and Carla Penny from the Department of Social Security, here to see Mr Jones.'

Syd slammed the door. '*Shit.*'

'What's the bloody racket?' said Dad.

'Social!'

'*Shit.*' Dad was out of the bedroom as quick as his load-bearing legs could manage. 'Move the baccy. Move the bloody baccy.'

They both scrambled to get the stash back into the bedroom, the sound of frustrated bangs on the door. It was like watching two ants scurrying from a boiling kettle. Bundles of baccy seemed to fly in all directions, as did many swear words. Some minutes' chaos saw most of the stuff thrown out of sight, Dad left Syd and wobbled into the living room. I followed, strangely entertained, and watched him collapse into his chair.

'Is it clear Syd?' he said, interspersed with several panting episodes.

"ang on...' The bedroom door slammed. 'Clear!'

Dad practised his 'ridden with arthritic pain' face. Satisfied, he then bawled to Syd. 'OK. Let 'em in.'

The front door was opened to disgruntled mumbles.

'Soz,' said Syd. 'I was just, er, cleanin' up a bit for Mr Jones.'

They stepped into the living room, which was as clean as a bin.

'Mr Jones?' A man with a side parting strode forward. 'Department of Social Security. You'll have had a letter about our visit.' There was a badge on his white shirt which advanced the information 'Home Liaison Co-ordinator'.

Dad grunted.

'My name is David Owen and this is Carla Penny – who I believe you've met before. We're here to talk about your disability benefit.'

I looked at the pretty lady, her poise demur, perhaps trying to find a foothold in her first job.

And another low cut top! Now I remember...

'Sit down,' said Dad.

The settee was sufficiently dirty for them to remain standing.

'So Mr Jones,' said David Owen, 'How is the arthritis?'

Dad shrugged. 'So so. Good days and bad days.'

'Yes, I believe it was a bad day on Carla's last visit.'

The pretty lady remained a step behind her colleague, yet stood firm.

Dad looked at her. 'Yeh, that was a bad day.'

'I'll cut to the chase Mr Jones – as you'll be aware, there's been a very serious allegation made against you.'

'All lies.'

'Well, that's what we're trying to determine.'

'Determine what you like – it's still bullshit.'

David Owen cleared his throat and a probing finger itched beneath his collar. 'OK Mr Jones,' he said, 'let me just ask you outright. Have you ever, whilst claiming disability allowance, systematically targeted each residential home within the West Hull area offering bootlegged tobacco as, quote: "shit that makes you better"?'

Dad grunted.

'Pardon?'

'It's an insult.'

'I'm not here to play games Mr Jones. I suggest you answer me.'

'Bollocks.'

'Is that "no"?'

'Yeh.'

'With regards to your benefit claim Mr Jones, without sufficient help you are house bound?'

'Yeh.'

'And that's how the situation remains?'

'Yeh.'

'I see. Is there anything you'd like to add?'

'Not really.'

'Well, Mr Jones. I'm afraid we have compelling evidence to the contrary.'

Dad looked away. 'You're just full of bollocks kid.'

David Owen placed a briefcase neatly on the floor and removed a file. A smile tickled his lips as he handed it to Dad. 'Please look carefully Mr Jones. The photograph is dated a week ago.'

I moved to peer over Dad's shoulder, as did Syd.

Inside the file, there was a photo that showed Dad leaving the Parkview residential home with a holdall over his shoulder – the only thing missing was for him to have a fistful of banknotes.

Get out of that one, you fat bastard.

'It's a fake,' Syd blurted, ''e was w'me last week.'

'Impossible, sir.'

'No way – we've been shiftin' it down the market since last Wednesd'y.'

Nice one Syd.

'In actual fact sir, the photograph was taken last Monday.' David Owen sniffed and removed a notepad from his briefcase. 'Would that have been the Walton Street Market, sir?'

Syd was quiet.

Dad's face reminded me of when I caught him licking the frying pan clean. 'Bollocks. It's all bollocks.'

'Mr Jones, your questionable disability and extra income are serious matters indeed.'

We all knew Dad was done for, I was probably glad. David Owen moved closer, as if for the kill. The pretty lady stood firm.

'Mr Jones, I must now caution you…'

Dad screamed and grasped his leg.

'Mr Jones?'

'It's flaring up.'

'I beg your pardon?'

'My arthritis!'

'I see,' said David Owen, scribbling something on his notepad.

Dad wailed like a sprog, though no-one seemed particularly bothered. He waved his arms at me. 'Get my pills, son. Quick!'

The room waited for my reaction.

After a while, I said: 'You having Mum back then?'

'What? What you on about? Pills!'

'Answer the question.'

'I'm in agony.'

'Say you'll talk to her.'

'Did I bring you up to be such a tosspot? Eh? If you've got one ounce of sense in that bonehead of yours, go and get my bleeding pills.'

'And Mum?'

'She can whistle.'

Why the hell did I ever put up with you?

Dad continued to rant. 'Do you speak English? *Get my pills.*'

I followed his command and left in search.

A moment later, I returned to the party. At the centre of the room and the centre of attention, I dropped an armful of baccy on the floor. 'The bedroom's full of it,' I said.

It was quiet, so quiet I could hear next door's telly.

'Bastard!' Dad bawled. 'I'll have you for this. I'll have you...'

I set off home.

'Don't forget, Ginger,' Syd called after me, 'Frid'y night, the marina. It's gonna be *big* – if y've got the bollocks for it.'

Bollocks? I've got plenty, you cunt.

I kept walking.

There was a phone box at the top of my street. Inside, I rummaged through my pockets and pulled out a small card, dialling the number with strong prods.

I heard three rings before someone answered. 'Can I speak to Inspector Briggs please?' I said.

'I'm sorry,' said a woman, 'Inspector Briggs is unavailable. Can I take a message.'

'The marina, half eleven Friday night – *Lady of the Humber*. It's gonna be *big.*'

'I'm sorry?'

'Just tell him that.'

'Can I ask who it is calling?'

I hung up.

PART THREE

Nine days later

Sixteen

I am a fool,
that much is true.

Before long, the commotion of the robbery had eased and I dared think I could relax a little. As such, the days began to drag, and I took leave of one averagely miserable Monday morning, headed for The Pork Café. Mooching along Hessle Road, I negotiated Boyes department store and a throng of harshly faced, potbellied fishwives. By the Criterion pub, jaundiced veterans of the Cod Wars queued for eleven o'clock opening. I remembered seeing an old photo of Hessle Road, the scene peeled back by a hundred years. Then, aproned shopkeepers posed outside their establishments, proudly presenting their wares. Now, every façade drew attention to a particular discount, bargain, or saving – tat peddlers catering to the poverty line. Indeed, everyone was skint; beg, borrow and steal were mantras. But rather like the post Thatcher wastelands of South Yorkshire, the neighbourhood was congealed by defiance-in-defeat. The fishing industry may have been comprehensively fucked over, but 'Ull folk could still embellish benefit claims; bypass the electricity meter; and wipe their arses on council tax bills.

Anyway, passing the lepers emerging from the Marmaduke Health Centre, I hit a home straight to The Pork Café. In the window, grey nets sat behind the moniker of the place, stencilled in a semicircle and underlined by a string of sausages. Inside, Brian sat perusing the day's black pudding themed specials, his bronzed skin somewhat obvious amongst the pallor of the other patrons. I joined him.

'It is all very exciting, don't you think?' said Brian, a few minutes later. 'Somewhere the real robber is sprawled on a gorgeous beach, speedos, body glistening in the heat – and he's living licentiously on the money we and the company have worked hard for.'

I grinned. 'Worked hard?'

Brian gave a tut, producing a small padded envelope from somewhere beneath the table – though I was sure his trousers were far too tight to have concealed it. 'Before I forget, *this* arrived for you this morning.'

Distracted by the fresh highlights to his hair, I pulled a face. 'It came to the factory?'

'No chuck, I collected it from Narnia.' Brian delivered the envelope across the table and continued with a fresh voice. 'So, line dancing tonight?'

'Thanks, but I'm tweezing my nasal hair.'

The writing across the envelope was scraggly and appeared hurried, it taking a hard look to be readable. Inside was a matchbox – nothing else. So, I opened the matchbox, and beneath some grubby cotton wool, I found something hidden.

A ring.

'Ginger? What is it?'

Brian's voice faded into irrelevance. I could but stare at the ring, my guts feeling putrid. Reasonable comprehension left the building, my head a montage of excruciating memories.

A manicured hand snatched the matchbox. Across the table, Brian observed the contents. He jiggled about like a jester. 'Oh Ginger. For me? Such a big red stone and just my colour.'

I steadied a hand tremble. 'Listen—'
'I think we'll have a summer wedding...'
I stood.
'And we'll honeymoon somewhere liberal.'
I punched Brian in the face.

He yelped, flinging his arms, the chair toppled, sending an express delivery of melodrama to the floor. As he clambered back, our eyes caught – he covered his face, like a game of hide and seek. My throat was dry, words sticking like a chunk of carrot.

So, I took the ring and left.

Chas's ring spent the rest of the day buried in my pocket. I could hardly bring myself to look at it, and as I tried to grasp some logic, a plausible reason for why it had returned to haunt me, I found only cloudiness, of which a ring twinkled through, proud to be the instigator of torment.

Back home, Mum had news from the chip shop, news she felt had to be pelted towards me upon entrance. Chas, she said, had been arrested. Not only arrested, but arrested and charged on numerous class A drugs offences. But not only Chas, she said, his whole inner circle, including the elusive The Slap.

Then Mum said: 'Apparently there was a tip off, there was a raid on the marina late Friday night. Looks like someone's been a grass.'

My heart plummeted so deep I could have excreted it – I realised *I* was that grass.

Seventeen

You never look, so
you'll never know.

'Is the line dancing on tonight?'

A Kosovan Barman offered me a questioning stare.

'Line dancing?' I said.

He stared. 'Ah?'

'Oh for God's sake…'

I knew of no other pub like The Lion Hotel – the sticky carpet was almost like walking through water, the same water thinning the colour of the spirits, like the water absent from the plumbing of the urinals – my God the place reeked. Such an establishment had secured a loyal clientele by way of a liberal attitude to – shall we say – herbal cigarettes, corner of the lounge facilitating this. That and the fact it was the only place within miles to allow the lunacy of line dancing.

Lunacy that, looking around, appeared distinctly absent.

'*Upstairs!*' said a toothless crone, staring at me from the bar. 'Line dancing is upstairs my duckling.'

Pulling a face, I followed her directions, as I imagined her cackling and disappearing into a puff of smoke.

Up on the first floor, I could hear music. It was strange music, spilling through the floor above – not at all your average cowboy noise. A curling staircase took me closer, like that of a lighthouse, and then stopped abruptly. I was before a single door, from behind of which the music seemed to penetrate my chest with an electronic pulse. I stood still, then fidgeted, then banged on the door.

After a while, a hairy man in a leotard answered.

'Who are you?' he shouted over the music.

I looked at him, he intensified his frown. It was preposterous – black Lycra over gorilla-like hair, complemented by full beard. 'I'm Ginger,' I shouted back. 'Line dancing? Is this the place?'

'What's the magic word?' he said, scratching his left nipple.

I shrugged. 'Brian asked me to come.'

'Brian, eh?' He took a good eyeful of my existence, sniffed and then disappeared into the music.

Tentatively, I stepped inside.

Judging by the booming music and artillery fire pyrotechnics, I found myself inside some sort of party – though an insatiable taint to the atmosphere made me nervous.

Hang on, that man's wearing a tool belt... And he's kissing a man dressed as a woman. Jesus! Doesn't that create a wormhole or something?

As I glanced around, I was really quite staggered – behind the bar, a man wore nothing but a collar and a thong, two ladies – *are they ladies?* – danced, probing one another intimately – and I was sure the dimly lit corners disguised misdemeanours I was grateful for not seeing.

A man in a leather mask approached, the pace too brisk for comfort – his mouth unzipped:

'Ginger?'

I froze. 'Look, I'm just here for...'

'Ginger, it's me.' The mask pulled up from his face, resting upon his head like a baby bottle teat.

'Brian!'

Frowning, his manicured finger brought to my attention a bugger of a black eye. 'How else should I cover up *this?*'

I glanced away.

'Why are you here?'

I wanted to tell him 'sorry', but I didn't.

'You want to go somewhere quieter?'

'Yeh,' I mumbled.

So Brian led the way. I followed him across the room, head down, pushing my way through the sexual equivalent of liquorice all-sorts.

'What's your problem?' he said, closing us in a small room. He perched upon a grotty sofa and peered across the room to me. 'Have you got something to say?'

The floorboards creaked as I fidgeted.

'Well?'

'I'm sorry – about your eye. I'm sorry.'

'Do I get an explanation?'

Seeing Brian sat there, leather pants and topless – it was just so unsettling. I grasped for something to say. 'Line dancing? It's not what I thought.'

His voice warmed a little. 'After hours – just a small group of us. We've got to the regional finals.'

There was a pause.

'Brian…' I said, sounding kind of coy. 'That ring… Well it's *that* ring.'

'You mean "The Ginger-Jones-gripe-with-life-poor-me-never-ending-moan" ring?'

'Yeh,' I mumbled – *but can't we just call it a ring?* I dug into my pocket and passed it over to him.

'Hmm.' His eyes appeared keen, almost greedy. 'Not cheap I'll bet. Do you know who sent it?'

'Chas… Maybe…'

'Well who else?'

'Did you see anyone? Anything unusual at the factory?'

'No.' He shrugged. 'So just give it back – *again*.'

'I can't,' I snapped. 'Chas is banged-up. He's been done for drugs and it's *my* fault – I grassed him.'

'*You?*'

'I found out, by accident really – I wasn't thinking... Look, Brian, will you take it, hide it.'

'Why would I do that?'

'No-one knows about you, you'd be safe, no-one would know.'

'Like hell.'

'I can't go through this again.'

'Just this morning, *chuck*, you walloped me in the face.'

'And I'm sorry, really. But please take it. It'd just be until...' My sentence petered to a whimper.

'You stupid bastard,' said Brian, following through with a protracted exhalation. He offered a half smile, though I perceived the sentiment similar to pity sex. 'Maybe, if it's just... only until you sort things. Temporary foster care, that's all.'

Two men entered the room in haste, joined at the mouth like Siamese twins.

Yikes!

'Excuse me.' Brian scowled. 'Engaged!'

For a moment, they parted. One giggled, the other shrugged – and they fondled heavily as they left. Outside, a car passed by, awkwardness making the sound very interesting indeed.

'So,' said Brian a while later. 'It seems all you can do is sit tight.'

'Don't tell anyone about this,' I said, looking away as he tucked the ring into some fold of his leather pants. 'I need to get my head straight.'

'Fine.' He continued with a brighter voice, though it sounded forced: 'Listen chuck, fancy a drink?'

In turn, I forced a smile. 'Why not.'

Back at the party, we squeezed our way through sweaty bodies, ending by the bar. I stood with my arms folded, a little more at ease in my protective huddle. Brian's presence seemed to command prompt service, and he placed in front of me a tall glass containing a kind of gloopy concoction. I tasted through a straw, tentatively.

I nodded. 'Nice.'

'It's one of our special cocktails,' said Brian.

'What's it called?'

'A Cock Sucking Bandit.'

With that, I made an excuse and left.

Two days later

Eighteen

I'll squeeze every inch
of your pitiful life.

As I left Redbourne Street Police Station, answering bail had made me feel like a white, less murderous O.J. Simpson – that lived in 'Ull. I knew only that the investigation was ongoing, and that I should answer extended bail in a couple of weeks. I found this quite unsatisfactory and considered a formal complaint; but then I remembered the wad of cash inside my toilet tank, and thought it best I didn't push my luck. Indeed, despite the tease, I dared not disturb the swag nor chance thoughts on how to spend it – a bit like the ring thing really.

'Taxi for Ginger?'

Across the street, my eyes were drawn to a black cab, engine chugging like a tractor. The driver caught my glance and our eyes held for long enough to make it exceedingly awkward if I walked on. His arm hung lazily from the window, slapping the door panel like a letch on a hooker's arse.

'Come on then pal, chop chop,' he said, his voice hoarse. 'Meter's on.'

I shook my head. 'Not for me.'

'You're Ginger?'

I nodded.

'Then I'm at your service, pal. Prepaid.'

Assuming that police bail came with a free ride, I shrugged, trotted across the road and climbed into the back. 'Can you take me to—'

Without warning, the doors locked and the cab took off, tipping me across the backseat.

'St. George's Road please,' I said, straightening myself up.

The driver shifted through the gears, a moment in the rear-view mirror showing him as middle-aged and rough looking in a shaven head kind of way. 'The back seat – there's a letter,' he said flatly.

On such prompting, I noticed a folded sheet of A4 resting beside me – inside I found a photograph. The image elicited a retch and conjured such emotion that I felt dizzy. The photo was of me, in a bloody heap by the railway sidings. The reverse read in bold capitals: REMEMBER? As a paralysis held body and mind, the universe seemed to pause and my existence became vacuous. My eyes were fixed, taking multiple snapshots of the photo and feeding the exposures into my head. Each mental representation renewed the pain, as though being punched and kicked by the invisible man. I vomited, and it projected over the back seat – bilious and absent of chunk, it seeped into the upholstery to leave nothing more than a shadow.

'Oi,' said the driver, his eyes wide in the rear-view mirror. 'That's a standard thirty quid clean-up charge.'

Folding out the sheet of A4, I found within my grasp an HMP Visitation Pass for Hull Prison, prisoner name: Charles Holder.

My nausea returned. 'What does he...' I abandoned the question, reckoning the answer to be inescapably bleak.

'Just doin' me job pal, that's all,' said the driver, peering into the rear-view mirror. Such indifference seemed thinly veiled, a menace to his eyes suggesting he'd have been ready to bundle me into the cab regardless of my co-operation.

I closed my eyes, trusting only in my most basic of instincts – to survive.

I squinted through the streaky window. An enigma of spalling Victorian walls seemed to wrap around the cab, behind the moss of which I could easily imagine rapists playing ping-pong. Inside, I was shown to a table, in a room, watched over by many suspicious eyes. I squirmed as all around me more people came, sat at tables and gazed into oblivion with the same absence. In single file, the rogues entered. Some of them were huge tattooed brutes that shook the ground as they marched to their loved ones; others were small, slimy and seemed to leave a trail across the room. So, as I sat there, around me lovers touching and cherishing what little time they had, I happened upon my own reunion. A man was sitting before me. He wasn't a loved one – he was a cunt. Perhaps there was someone, somewhere, who wanted to touch him, but that person wasn't here. Just me. And I judged him a cunt.

Chas stared at me. His face was red, moulded to fit a frown that was rigid and I reckoned had been permanent for many weeks. I looked back at him, glancing away when our eyes held. He seemed less, I mean physically there was less of him, his barrel shaped body drained by a good few pints.

'There's lots of people I can't trust,' he said.

I paused. 'I, er, I don't understand…'

'Can I trust you?'

He means the ring, right? He must mean the ring. Fuck what do I say? How do I… 'But why? I mean… Why did—'

'Can I *trust* you?'

Nervousness set in like Parkinson's, and I nodded like the dog in the back of Uncle Ray's car.

'That's good.'

I plucked a little courage. 'I don't want... like before...'

'Behave yourself and there'll be no problem.'

'Right.'

'How's Morris?' he croaked, like there was a breeze block in his throat.

'Dad? He's, er, OK... I think.'

'How's he coping with the split? They'd been together a good few years, right?'

'Well, I... er, I don't see that much of him.'

'That's good. He's a parasite.'

'How did you...?'

'I pick things up. I hear your old lady's staying with you?'

I nodded.

'Must be cosy.'

'Not exactly.'

'Too much gob – she drives Leon mad down the fish restaurant.'

If Chas was capable of smiling, the facial twitch I then witnessed was one such expression. It quickly vanished.

'You see much of Syd?' he said.

'No.'

'Does a bit of bootlegging for your old man I hear?'

I shrugged. 'I don't see him – neither of them.'

'I reckon I can understand that. He betrayed you.'

I looked away – recollecting was still painful.

'Look kid, I'm making no apologies. I needed you here, so I pulled a dirty trick. Believe me, I've done much worse.' He cleared his throat. 'But it's in the past now – it's *all* in the past.'

'Why am I here?' I said, tentatively.

Chas took a deep breath. 'You know what happened to me?'

I nodded.

'I was betrayed too.'

If only he knew – I couldn't keep eye contact.

'You're here to help me with something.'

'Me?'

He moved in close and lowered his voice. 'Someone grassed.' Chas's face had reddened, almost enough to do away with the lights. 'Five people knew about the marina that night – no-one else. Four of that five are in here – a couple more of my lads on Micky Mouse shit. Nearly everyone who works for me has had the pigs up their arses – except one. That one knew about the marina, he knew everything. The voice of reason tells me the other lads wouldn't rat on themselves – if this sticks we're facing a lot of years. So that leaves one: the one who knew it all yet gets no bother.' His breath was heavy on my face. 'What does that say to you?'

'I'm glad I'm not that one.'

'So guess who.'

'I don't... er...'

Chas almost spat at me: 'Sydney Clough.'

'Syd?'

'I thought he'd bottled it that night – decided he was out of his depth. No. He was down the pigs spewing out.' He inhaled like a solvent abuser. 'And you know the worst insult?'

I shook my head.

'Before it kicked off, I'd trusted Syd with Ma's ring.'

What?

'Trusted him to keep it from prying eyes. And now he double-crosses me.'

So Syd sent me the ring?

'If he thinks he's found a pot of gold at the end of the rainbow...'

And I passed it to Brian.

'...He'll see soon enough that *I* don't take that kind of disrespect.'

Why the hell did I bring Brian into this? It's such a mess! I can't think... 'OK,' I said, 'Well... thanks for letting me know...'

'Sit down!'

I sat.

'Listen.'

I listened.

'I want you to find Syd.'

That's not so bad.

'Take back what's mine.'

So I go see Brian, get the ring and then tell a few fibs…

'And then take *away* the problem.'

OK, that is bad.

'Pardon?' I mumbled.

'*Take care of it.*' Chas's voice scraped my spine and jabbed each vertebrae on the way.

I stared at him.

'The pigs are on my lads day and night – I can't risk it. It's a matter of trust and I'm putting that trust in you. You're a lucky lad.'

Yes, I've really hit the jackpot.

'I'll see you all right – don't worry about that.'

'But *me?*… I mean, I'm not…'

'I need it safe. Simple. You minded it before – if *I* struggled for it you must have something about you. Besides, you *owe* Syd. Am I right?'

I shut my eyes. I couldn't comprehend what was being asked of me, it seemed surreal. Nothing could have prepared me for such a smack in the face. In fact, I would have preferred a smack in the face.

'I can't… I mean…' I took a long, deep breath. 'What if?'

'If?'

I spilled the words quickly. 'If I can't do it – if I *won't* do it?'

It was quiet for a moment.

'I think we've been there before kid.'

Indeed we had, I wasn't keen on going back.

I opened my eyes and stared into nothing. Chas spoke and I grunted intermittently, God only knows what he was saying, what I agreed to. I was drowned in thought yet I couldn't tell a single one. Seconds passed, minutes, perhaps hours. All I knew was that my head was in a bad place.

Soon, a screw called out we had five minutes left. The room was again reality and there became a busyness. Goodbyes stained the air with snot and the occasional escaped tear. There was a loud sobbing, in particular. Accentuating, it made the people mumble, and I followed the room's attention to see a man, hands clasped with an older lady, openly crying like a child.

It was The Slap.

I gawped. He was like a balloon model, but made from muscle sausages, and seeing this huge, hairless lump blubbering so – it was really shocking.

After a while Chas said: 'Can't cope – seeing his nan. Too much shame.'

I looked at him.

'She brought the kid up – mother never wanted to know.'

I could have felt sad – but I didn't.

And so time was called. Goodbye slobbers preceded slow, clingy exits. Goodbye punches preceded quick, obscenity driven ejections. Everyone avoided The Slap like he was syphilis.

We became the last dregs. Chas helped four screws prise The Slap from his nan – I would have been embarrassed had I not a sack of woe. The struggle faded and the room held three.

'Come on Chip Shop – you too,' said a screw.

Chas glanced back and pointed at me. 'Be clever.'

I looked up, but said nothing.

Nineteen

Whatever I wish,
it smells of fish.

I'd never been a huge drinker. A few bottles of Newcastle Brown once taught me I could long-jump the length of a Ford Sierra; and then a kebab taught me I could vomit the length of three. This had warranted selective abstinence, but that night, like many other lonely, woeful people on the planet, my despairing moments were accompanied by a massive intake of alcohol. I staggered about town, hugging my bottle of cider like it was precious pornography. Incapacity kidded me into thinking a two litre bottle of White Strike had simply made me 'merry', and as such, I found myself kicking at the front door of a house. Before long, there was light, an open widow, and someone shouting from the house over the fence.

'What business have you here?' said a woman, the bedroom behind glowing a kind of brothely-pink.

I burped in her direction. 'Business of the mind your own sort.'

'I'm calling the police!'

'No-one's in,' I said.

There was a pause, before she screamed at me: 'That's the shed you twat.'

I had wondered why someone had a ride-on mower in their front room. I pressed my face against the window. It was a very big shed, bigger than my bedsit. I considered this – I reckoned I could have lived happily in such a shed.

You see, unlike the streets/landfills I was accustomed to walking, I found myself in a place where dog shit was scooped and the street lights didn't flicker. Had I not been intoxicated, I would have noticed a very large house next to the lawnmower shed, I would have noticed the Lexus in the drive, and I would have noticed the empty swimming pool I then fell into.

Failing that, I would have definitely noticed the 'beware of dog' sign, I would have noticed the growling, and I would have noticed the saliva strung fangs as I clambered up.

The dog bit me and I fell back in.

I screamed like a girl, clasping my hand tight to my chest. Intoxication numbed me a little, and as the pain subsided, so too my wails faded into the cold night air. I slumped in the swimming pool – the barking above me was incessant and the dog's heavy breath created a mist that hung overhead. I simply sprawled over the bottom. Seconds became minutes became a smear of time. High up, the night sky was clear, glittering – I was sure I saw a shooting star. I made a wish, though alas, a kebab remained elusive.

'Don't move you little shit!' A voice cut the air with a horrible shrill: 'Don't speak, and don't think I won't chop you up.'

My bleary eyes fixed on a half-naked girl – wielding a garden spade. Beside her, the dog growled, as if performing a duet.

'Fancy the Lexus do you?' she yelled, struggling to keep the towel covering her modesty. 'Suzi likes chewing on testicles.' The dog barked in reply. 'And she'll enjoy shitting you out in the neighbour's flower bed.'

Notwithstanding the eroticism of flushed female flesh clutching a long wooden handle, the situation was potentially quite serious. I reckoned a sharp spade could equal a sharp scream – and hardly orgasmic. There were two reasons for my casual sprawling. Firstly, I was drunk – which is self-explanatory; and secondly, the realisation of where I was, what I was doing there, and whom was threatening me was battling such drunkenness.

'Look at me!' said the girl.

I obeyed.

'You may speak before Suzi eats you.'

I paused. 'Hello Ms Fish.'

It was quiet.

'What?' she said.

'It's me.'

She squinted. 'Just who the hell are you?'

'I need help,' I said.

'I beg your pardon?'

'A gun.'

'It's *you*.'

Me indeed.

'You look like a tramp... and you're *drunk*. Just wait until I tell Daddy.'

'Shall I put on a tie?'

'Get out of my pool!'

I struggled to move, but could manage no more than a slump.

'Get out of here – I never want to see you again.'

'Help me.'

'Use the steps you shit.'

I felt a lump in my throat. 'Help me.'

'Speak up!'

A tear tickled my cheek. 'I don't know what to do.'

'Try a shower.'

And so the feeble grip I held over my emotion was relinquished – I cried like a snotling.

'What's the matter with you? Get a grip.'

'I don't want to kill him.'

'What?'

'I can't – I won't.'

Ms Fish lowered her spade. 'I don't understand. Stop blubbing.'

'Scare him away – maybe I could tell him to go away and never come back. No-one'd know.'

'Scare who?'

'Help me.'

'How?'

'Get me a gun.'

'Pardon me?'

'A gun!'

'I wouldn't know how.'

'Lying bitch.'

'Don't you dare—'

'You're a *lying bitch*.'

'Enough. Get off my property.'

'Fuck you. You don't own me.'

She scrunched up her face, pointing the spade. 'Give me one reason why I shouldn't do you in right now.'

'Because you don't know who I've told.'

It fell so quiet I could almost hear the stars twinkle – even the dog stopped growling.

'Pardon?'

'You heard.'

She forced a laugh. 'Don't you dare threaten *me*.'

'No threat. Just cashing in a favour.'

'I owe you nothing.'

'I know what you did.'

'What we *both* did. I'll just take you down with me.'

'And what have *I* got to lose eh?'

The whole world seemed to pause for a moment. Her eyes

betrayed the threatening stance, I could see she was worried. I glared at her, my wet eyes stinging in the night air. I simply waited, before she spat the words at me:

'So what do you want?'

Twenty

Like what you see?
Well it don't come free.

The following morning, I awoke to a room that smelt of sick. I reckoned it was my own sick because it matched the taste in my mouth. The room was frilly, with pink drapes and such shit – which somehow made the sick smell worse.

Ms Fish was standing at the bottom of my huge, absorbing king sized bed. 'You're cleaning that up,' she said, pointing to a pebble dashed mirror, and then further chunks on the carpet.

'I need a drink.'

'Fuck you.'

She left a bucket and gloves on the dressing table.

What? No kiss?

Firstly, I found a bathroom and spent a couple of minutes swigging from the tap. Then, I swilled my mouth with Listerine and took a shower. The smell of food tingled my nasal passage, grooming my hung-over state into following.

Many rooms, halls and disgustingly overpriced interiors later, I found the kitchen. It was a big kitchen, not only bigger than my bedsit, but probably my street. Ms Fish was fiddling, unenthusiastically, around a big range-like cooker – she stopped and glared at me.

'Have you cleaned it?'

'Yes,' I said.

'Then sit.'

By the window, a gargantuan table displayed a single placemat at seat number twelve, which I then occupied. The table was unblemished, and I got the impression I was the first person to ever sit there. Indeed, the whole kitchen seemed like a pristine B&Q mock-up.

'I made you this,' said Ms Fish, offering a plate loaded with overdone chips. 'And then I remembered you're a cunt.' She snatched back, smiled and tipped the chips out of the window.

Glancing out over football pitches of garden, the autumn colours seemed to scream under a blue sky – I imagined the chips payment to a gardener who worked for food scraps. 'Nice day,' I said.

'Cut the crap.'

'Fine... Who shall I tell first?'

'Seriously, *that's* still your play? You're sounding tiresome.'

I shrugged. 'So where's "Daddy"?'

'Why would you care?'

'I don't.'

She placed her hands on her hips. 'He's recuperating with a *lady friend.*'

'Cosy.'

'She's a slut.'

I dared to laugh. 'I'm hungry. Where do we go for food?'

'We? Hardly.'

'And I need some fresh air. Do you like the seaside?' I paused to remember Scarborough, February 1986, gale force winds, a pink bucket and spade, alone on the beach and forsaken by Dad in favour of nine pints of Guinness – I reckoned it was time to overwrite that memory. 'What about fish and chips? It'll be a novelty for you.'

'I am aware of the concept,' she snapped.

'Great. Get your coat.'

Hell, she drove fast. She propelled the Lexus along the country roads with an utter disregard, seemingly for everything in the world, let alone me. At times I thought I noticed the wide eyed gormless smirk of a joyrider.

'Does this make you nervous?' she said.

'Not at all,' I replied, fear making me sound like a helium junkie.

'I could crash this car – kill the both of us. What then?'

I reckoned she enjoyed manicures too much. 'Please yourself.'

We got faster, as though to outrun a coyote with a stick of TNT. Men, women and children fled for their lives, but as we slowed a little for the streets of Sunny Scarborough, Ms Fish reckoned the death count to be no more than a hedgehog.

I say Sunny Scarborough, meaning it was cloudy and cold. Ms Fish drove along the promenade, and I remembered what the seaside was all about – a choppy sea, flashing amusements and the smell of fish and chips. She parked on a double yellow and we took a stroll. Amongst the people, candy floss and bingo calling, I felt a million miles away, almost secure. It was nice.

After a while Ms Fish said: 'So who knows?'

Reality sapped away any false comfort. 'Someone… Maybe no-one.'

'Bluster.'

'You reckon?'

'I eat guys like you with a side salad. You're a chancer – I won't give a penny.'

'I'm not interested in your money.'

'Are you still drunk?'

We walked, glancing at the sea, a dirty postcard – sporadic eye contact seemingly a blink-off.

'Do you propose some kind of arrangement?' said Ms Fish.

'What I said to you last night – I meant it.'

'How so?'

'I want a gun.'

She laughed. 'What the hell for?'

'For personal use.'

'Don't be ridiculous.' Ms Fish grabbed my arm, steering us until the people thinned away – we stopped by the sea wall. 'That's crazy. I can't help you.'

'You *will* help, though,' I said.

'Are you going to make me?'

'If I have to.'

Looking out, the sea seemed so vast and undiscovered, and as each wave enveloped the next, I fancied life would be easier if the sea enveloped *me*.

'I can stop your wages in a heartbeat.'

'But you won't.'

'Oh?'

'You're scared of me. You don't know me – and you can't figure balls from bullshit.'

Ms Fish wore a burgundy pea coat, from inside of which she produced a small dictation machine. 'So to clarify,' she smiled, pointing it to my face, 'why do you want a gun, exactly?'

I was quiet.

'And what will you do to *me*, a law abiding citizen, when I refuse to be drawn in?'

'Switch it off.'

She stepped back. 'Touch me – I'll scream.'

'In other news,' I said loudly. 'The Choice Seafood Robber has been revealed—'

A click from the machine cut me short, Ms Fish tucking said contraption back into her coat pocket. 'I've caught the juicy bits. Just to even the balance.'

As she turned, a rogue wave spilled over the wall, drenching her swank. She shrieked, I grabbed her from behind, a second wave then drenching us both. My hand slipped beneath her coat, across her chest and into her pocket. I tossed the dictation machine over the sea wall.

The freezing water made me gasp, but I smirked. 'How's the balance sitting now?'

She shoved me into a stumble. 'Get me a fucking towel!'

Grasping a cup loaded with twenty-pence pieces, my feet squelched across the arcade to a table in the shape of a fishing boat.

'What did you order?' said Ms Fish, beach towel draped over her shoulders. The transparency of her damp blouse accentuated her bra and the eye-poppers held within.

I plonked myself beside her. 'Shit on a stick.'

'Prick. Where's my change?'

I rattled the cup, then nodded toward a labyrinth of arcade games.

'Seriously?'

The amusements into which we'd retreated offered a small nautical themed café, tucked in between the bingo and shoot-'em-ups, warm air from the deep fryer served to re-heat our cockles.

A while later, Ms Fish looked up from her mug of tea and said: 'Why me? *You* must know a thousand scallywags.'

I shrugged. 'The theft of fifty grand, the attempted murder of a security guard—'

'Keep it down, buster.' She kicked my shin beneath the table. 'Anyhow, that man's alive. So it was hardly an accomplished attempt.'

I spoke with restraint. 'An accomplished attempt would *be* murder.'

'Stop splitting hairs. There's a lack of evidence and people know not to blab.'

'So the security bloke saw you?'

'That perverted sleazebag won't dare open his mouth.' She kicked me again. 'Nor will you.'

Or what? Talk and I get a fish head in my bed?

I made for the nearest game and slipped in a couple of coins. A burst of light and electronic ditty saw a Wild West apocalypse unfold before me – I took aim of a cowboy zombie with my Uzi.

'What's your name?' said Ms Fish.

Eat lead zombie! No brains for you today. 'I told you – people just call me Ginger.'

'Rubbish. Your *real* name.'

Ginger was all I'd known since being a sprog. If my real name was shouted in the street I would never turn my head. 'Lloyd,' I mumbled quickly. 'Like the bank.'

'Lloyd's not so bad. What's the big deal?'

Jesus, I'm trying to kill zombies here! 'Nothing. Until you know it was to remind Dad to keep up the loan repayments.'

Ms Fish released a long sigh. 'Lloyd, if I help you, there'll be conditions.'

I glanced to her.

'Whatever you're planning, I have to be in too.'

'No way.'

'*Way*. You've got something on me, now I need to have something on *you*. If you rat on me, I can rat on you too. Get it?'

Game over! Thanks a lot, bitch. 'I'm not having you take over,' I said, dropping my Uzi like a spent Twix wrapper.

'Do you think you can come and threaten me on a whim?'

'This is… different.'

'Look, I help you. Then we never speak or see each other again.' She sniffed, it somehow sounding begrudging. 'If that's not acceptable, and you *still* insist on being a tell-tale tit… I guess we go to jail.'

'But I don't trust you.'

She flicked her hair. '*Ditto.*'

With no thoughts more cunning, I concocted a version of the truth: 'OK. I need to scare someone,' I said. 'I mean *really* scare him. So he leaves and never comes back.'

'Who? Why?'

'I can't tell you that.'

'But he'd have to be *really* scared – utterly shitless. Even then, how could you guarantee he'd disappear?'

'Well… I can't…'

'Then we need a plan.'

I pulled a face. 'All *you* need to do is get what I asked for.'

'I hope you realise that gun wasn't real?'

'What?'

'A replica, I bought it through an associate of an associate.'

'It looked real to me.'

'That's the point.'

I shrugged. 'It's not like I was actually going to shoot him anyway.'

Ms Fish observed me for a moment. 'Well, quite.'

Fish and chips arrived at the table, and as I sat beside Ms Fish, the waitress's raised eyebrow and short glance back were perhaps an indicator that we looked suspicious.

'I'll give you my number,' said Ms Fish. 'You can loan my second mobile – call when you're ready.'

I nodded.

'But only then. Don't think we're friends or anything.'

Looking down, I picked at my food, passing the odd stealthy glance towards Ms Fish. When I imagined us together, naked, writhing – it gave me a tingle.

'So what's *your* name?' I said quickly, without looking up.

'Arabella,' she replied – there was no emotion.

'That's nice.'

'I know. Anything else?'

Er… There must be something else I can say…

I sighed, then we finished our lunch and went home.

Twenty-One

I can smile inside, now that
I know I don't have to be you.

The Nokia 5110 was my very first mobile phone. Loaned from Ms Fish to call her as appropriate, it also facilitated a form of witchcraft known as SMS. Against my better judgement, I had given the number to Brian.

Hi Ginger. Hows u? Bri.

OK. Is ring Ok?

U not trust me? Lol. It safe.

Might need it soon.

? Sure U OK?

Yes.

U want to chat?

No.

☹

It had been a week since my meeting with Ms Fish – a Thursday night to be specific – and Mum was down the Chinese with *my* money. My intention was to sit and mull, but I had a visitor. The person to whom I answered the front door was unexpected, to say the least.

'Dad?'

'I wanna see Mum.'

'She's out.'

'Then I'll wait.' He accepted his own invitation to come in, plonked himself on my bed and breathed heavily. 'We've things to say.'

Dad looked as though he'd stopped ten yards from dropping dead. 'You walked?' I said.

He nodded.

'You're too fat.' I looked at him hard. *You are too fat – but you've lost weight. Yes, there's definitely less of you.* 'You on a diet?' I said.

He shook his head.

We were a good minute into each other's company and he hadn't yet called me an idiot, or a twat, or a dickhead.

'So what's up with you?' I said.

Dad took a moment to steady his breath. 'I've come to claim her.'

'Mum?'

'For what she's worth.'

I didn't know what to say really. 'Suppose you'd better wait then.'

'Ta.'

He sat there, kind of lost, there was a first day at school look about him. He also looked dirty, smelt nasty and had a pallor that suggested he had the same attitude towards vegetables as he had God – they didn't exist.

I considered my betrayal of him and couldn't help but sigh. If he'd have seemed as pathetic then I probably would have played the game – and saved us *all* a lot of trouble.

'What happened with Social?' I said.

'I'm in court in a fortnight.'

'Oh.'

Dad didn't seem particularly angry, more resigned to his fate.

'What's going to happen?'

'Get a fine, probably lose most of me benefit. I won't go down though.'

'Well… suppose that's something.'

'Yeh.'

It was quiet for a moment.

'How's stuff then?' I said.

'Been better.'

'Yeh, daft question really.'

'Yeh.'

'You want a drink or something?'

'No.'

I had little else to say to Dad, in fact I barely knew him.

'Does she talk about me much?' he said.

'A bit.'

'I thought she could come away for a few days, just the two of us. What do you think?'

'She's a bit unpredictable.'

He mumbled.

'What?'

'I'm lonely,' he said.

I looked at him, then walked into the kitchen to make a drink. I knew all about loneliness, growing up with shit parents. A nasty hollow feeling that disconnects you from everything, a feeling you could never properly capture with words, but then even if you could there'd be no-one to listen. I wanted to shout at Dad 'that's what it *feels* like,' but I didn't, I made myself a coffee.

Mum returned.

'A full hour for an omelette and bloody fried rice!' She slammed the door, her skinny hand clutching a large paper bag that was kind of a greasy see-through colour. She saw Dad, stopped, observed him for a moment and then carried on to the kitchen.

'Hello Eileen,' he said.

Mum ignored him.

'How are you?'

She took two plates from the draining board, wiping them clean with a piece of tissue from her pocket.

I nudged her. 'He's trying. Give him a chance.'

She kicked me in the shin. 'Touch me again and I'll batter you.'

'You look… well,' said Dad.

Mum looked like she always had – bony and haggard.

'I'll dish up,' I said. 'Go and sit down.'

She grumbled, occupied the only chair and turned her back on Dad.

'Still working at chip shop?' he said. 'I miss fish and chips. I aint had it since… you know.'

'Is that all you've got to say?' said Mum.

'What?'

'Fish and bloody chips!'

'Well…'

'Get out.'

'No, please, just listen to me.' Dad's voice was pleading, it didn't suit him – it embarrassed me.

'I'll give you five seconds.'

'I just want, I mean—'

'Four.'

'Ray on the second floor. He's got a caravan. He said we could have it for a few days. What do you say? We can talk things through?'

'Three.'

'It's on the same site we went for honeymoon. You remember? We ruled the dance floor that weekend! And the bingo? I clobbered that fella in the wheelchair?'

'Two.'

'Syd said he'll take us down, him and Mary'll look after the flat. You don't have to worry about a thing. No cooking or nowt. I've got a tonne of micro meals from Kwik Save.'

'One.'

'Eileen please!'

Dad sounded so pathetic, all his past arrogance and bloody-mindedness seemed like a memory of a different person.

Finally, Mum said: 'No.'

'Wait!' I was buggered if I was going to lose a chance of getting rid of them *both*. 'Mum you're *going*.'

'Or what?'

'Or you're out on the street.'

She sneered at me. 'You wouldn't dare.'

Gritting my teeth, I could feel my eyes bulge. 'Don't push it bitch.'

Mum's face contorted with an ambivalence suggesting she didn't know whether to cry or spit – she lit a fag.

'Not inside!'

Dad shouted back: 'Show Mum some respect!'

What? Like you?

Mum blew her smoke into my face, pointing with her fag. 'I don't know who you think you are.'

'He's *nowt*,' said Dad. 'That's who he is. Thinks he's some kind of big shot, now he's got his own place.'

I summoned a plethora of self-control. 'I just want you two back together.'

'Come on Eileen,' said Dad, rising to his full five-foot-four. 'One more chance. For the kids.'

For the fucking kids? Only nineteen years too late you fat cunt.

Mum gave a throaty cough, pulled a face and swallowed. 'I'll think about it.'

'Nice one,' said Dad, allowing a smile to awaken long redundant muscles. 'That's a bloody start.'

'But you have to change.'

'What? How?'

'It *all* needs to change.'

'Well, tell me.'

So she did. All the old bollocks about the old days, the dancing, courting, mischief, laughter, copulation and the prerequisite to seek, with urgency, a small blue pill. Ugh!

Dad listened, nodding occasionally, a mostly taut expression suggesting a degree of pain. After a while, he offered Mum's coat and suggested a drink at The Lion. She took a minute to take it from him, further wittering about what she expected in the future, but eventually they did leave together – Mum grunting a lot, Dad almost walking on tiptoes.

I flopped on my bed – I didn't care if Mum and Dad got back together – all I cared about was them buggering off and leaving Syd to flat sit. For those few days, I knew exactly where he would be.

I took a deep breath and called Ms Fish.

PART FOUR

Two days later

Twenty-Two

*I see you don't
look back with love.*

'OK with this?' I said, as the Lexus pulled up outside block 4.

Ms Fish tied her hair back, her petite ears begging me to nibble them. '*You're* the one who looks terrified.'

'I'm fine.'

Of course, I *was* terrified. To think that little more than a year ago I was an oik, and now I was a hired thug. I'd really come on in the world.

She frowned at me. 'And you can't wear *that* – I told you black.'

'It's all I could find.'

'How on earth did you think you could manage this on your own?' Ms Fish read from my T-shirt and looked at me with disbelief: '*Frankie says shit your pants.*'

I grunted.

'I have some spare things in the boot – you'll have to wear something of mine.'

'So where is it?' I said.

'Pardon?'

'You know...'

'No.'

'The gun!'

She gave a tut and lifted her black roll-neck. There, tucked neatly into her skinny waist, was a bloody gun. 'Do you approve?' she said.

'Yeh... I mean, you'd never tell.'

'What did you expect? A spud gun?'

I looked across the road, it was dark now and the street-lamps glowed in a damp reflection from the road. It had been a bugger of a day, raining incessantly. But now it had stopped, as it seemed had the world, in anticipation of our big performance.

'So,' said Ms Fish. 'I make the call, pretending to be...?'

'She was a one night stand from God knows how long ago – he won't remember what she sounds like.' I gave half a smile, then whispered instructions into her lovely ear.

Ms Fish handed me her mobile. 'I'd like to get this over with.'

I felt my heart move up a gear as I prodded in the number. 'Just make sure your voice is posh – even posh for you.'

As she waited for a reply, I moved in close.

'Hello. I want to speak to Syd.'

The phone spilled a tinny voice: 'Who is it?'

'Never you mind, madam. Just go and fetch him.' Ms Fish covered the mouth piece. 'It's a girl.'

'My sister,' I said. 'Syd's girlfriend.'

'You didn't tell me it was domestic.'

'I know.'

'Your family frolics are the last thing I need.'

'Too late.'

''ello. Syd 'ere,' said the phone.

'Er, yes, hello,' said Ms Fish. 'Is this Syd?'

'I just said that.'

'Yes, well, I would like a few words with you, mister.'

142

'Go on then.'

She paused, before announcing: 'I have borne you a girl.'

'What?' said the phone.

'I am the mother of your daughter.'

'Who is this?'

Ms Fish stalled.

'Rebecca,' I mumbled.

'Rebecca!'

'Who?'

'Pig! You break my heart.'

'I don't know any Rebecca.'

'Last year… a certain village bus shelter, a certain lack of contraception.'

There was a splutter of recognition.

'You said you loved me.'

''ow'd y'get this number?'

'Shut up and listen!' Ms Fish drenched the words with such indignation, she almost convinced *me*. 'I've waited a long time to track you down Syd. But now I know your friends, your family, your favourite jerk-off sock.'

'Just 'ang on a minute—'

'Flat 52, Block 4, your girlfriend has a brother named Ginger. I know *everything*.'

'But—'

'Be quiet! Meet me in fifteen minutes.'

'Y're a bloody loony.'

She gave a laugh worthy of a strait-jacket. 'Yes. And you'd better grow eyes in the back of your head.'

There was a deep, uncertain breath. 'Well… gimme an hour.'

'You make an excuse and meet me by the garages at the rear of your block.'

'But—'

'In *five* minutes.'

Ms Fish hung up.

I laughed. 'Pretty bloody good.'

She tightened the bun in her hair. 'Hmm. You think he'll come?'

'Oh yes.'

She mumbled, turned on the motor and drove us around the block.

Of the people living inside the tower block, there were few who could afford a car. Consequently, the row of garages Ms Fish and I hid behind was used for the bounties of house robbing, underage drinking and jacking up. The Lexus had been parked within one burnt-out example, just a few feet away, the black hole just perfect for concealing such an incongruous display of wealth.

I fidgeted. Ms Fish's polo neck itched like nothing else, as did the masks we both wore – we were the height of IRA fashion.

'It's too dark,' I said, peering across to the underpass. I was sure Syd should have emerged by now.

'It's been ten minutes. What do you suggest?'

A slither of red lipstick was visible from beneath her mouth-hole – it made me tingle. Even with the evil eyes of a terrorist balaclava, she looked kind of pretty. 'Couple more minutes,' I said. We stalked a while, then I mumbled: 'So what did you spend all that money on?'

'What's it to *you?*'

'Just wondered.'

Ms Fish thought for a second, seemingly to weigh up a reply. 'Things.'

'Like what?'

'I don't think I can remember.'

'Don't you ever get scared? I mean, *I* do.'

'Of what exactly?'

'Getting caught!'

'No.'

'I've still got that money you gave me. Too scared to spend it.'

'Your choice.'

'Suppose.'

'Nobody cares anymore – it's a piece of paper filed at the back of some inspector's draw. Daddy hardly needs the money. Just keep your mouth closed and forget about it.'

'But he's your dad. You screwed him over.'

'He'll live. He's got his slut to take care of him.'

'But…' I stopped as I remembered screwing over my own father. 'None of my business I suppose.'

'No.' She nudged me, speaking under her breath. 'Look.'

Approaching from the underpass was a figure, no more than a shadow. It was impossible to distinguish, until a street lamp flickered momentarily, the broken bulb giving enough light to reflect from two little round panes of – probably – bullet proof glass. I knew of no-one else with speccys so thick.

'It's Syd,' I said.

'Are you ready?'

I nodded.

Ms Fish crouched behind the side of the garage, as did I. Syd was in full view now, his skinny weasel-like treachery no less pungent. He paused, his eyes flicking over the surroundings, arms folded tight across his chest. He was clearly nervous and turned back on himself quickly, as if to catch a stalker.

One of those stalkers – Ms Fish that is – rose up and moved in from behind. I stayed still, a very scared kind of still.

'Sydney!' she said.

As he turned, she used the gun to clobber him in the face – he fell with a crack that made me shudder.

'W-what did you do that for?' I blurted, an octave over normal, totally unprepared for our felony.

'Pardon me? Did you think he would just climb into the boot of my car? Ask for some sweeties for the journey?'

Syd groaned, practically unconscious.

'No... I just...'

'Help me move him.'

We dragged his skin and bone back around to the concealed Lexus, he was so light I was scared he'd disintegrate in our hands. The boot took him comfortably, we tucked him in the corner, I tossed in his glasses, slamming the door on his groaning.

Tremulous hands removed my mask. Revenge wasn't sweet, more an adrenaline fuelled mush of emotion. But from the mess I grasped a thought that just seemed right. 'I wanna take him to the old sidings,' I said.

Ms Fish glared back from her knitted face. 'What? Where the hell is that?'

'Derelict platforms by the train station.' I restrained a shudder – any mention of the place was painful.

'No. We go to your bedsit. We agreed.'

'No you *told* me.'

She pulled up her mask. 'I'm quite sure I'm not going for a mystery tour with *that* in the boot.'

'It's *my* decision!'

She slapped me.

All my fear, uncertainty and frustration seemed to congeal into one knee-jerk reaction.

I slapped her back.

Ms Fish froze, I took a few clumsy steps backwards, my legs floppy, bowing under my weight. She strode forward, threw her face to mine.

And kissed me.

Bloody hell.

Of course, I kissed her back.

She hustled me back against the garage and we exchanged a good deal of saliva, before she pulled her head back and ran her finger tenderly over the lip she'd struck only seconds before. 'I made you bleed,' she said.

'I'll live.'

'Well?'

'Well what?'

She leered at me. Her hands moved over my chest and I shivered as she moved downwards.

I was so excited I was almost scared. 'Er…?'

'I'm only going down for ten seconds,' she said, kneeling before me, 'and if you haven't come you have to *beg* me to finish.'

Already she'd pulled me out and set to work. I held her head and moaned, my face tightly screwed as I lost myself. So often I had pondered happiness, how happiness had eluded me, teased me by others' zeal. Now, right there between my legs, I had happiness. *Oh God!* My pelvis jarred forward, my scrotum contracted: I couldn't contain it. A twitch deep inside, and abreast of a resonating wail, I let it out. I fell back against the garage, vaguely aware of Ms Fish somewhere close.

'How did I do?' I gasped.

There was a pause.

'Seven seconds – I think you have time for another.'

It was a nice thought, but – alas – the final three seconds simply passed.

Twenty-Three

Here we are deep in the night,
really is no time to fight.

It was 11:45 in the evening.

I fidgeted, the leather seat of Ms Fish's Lexus making a squeak. 'Do you fancy me?' I mumbled.

'Just keep your mind on what we've got to do please,' she said.

'That's it?'

She didn't reply – driving demanded intense concentration, apparently. The Lexus crept over the station car park, gliding over emptiness like socks over lino. A hole in the fence showed darkness behind, a darkness we couldn't turn back from, that we moved towards. I knew I was shaping my future, many years consequential of one night's activity. Syd, Chas, The Slap, Mum and Dad – everyone – my life had come to one point, *this* point.

'Put on your balaclava,' said Ms Fish, pulling down her own mask. '*I* do the talking – like we discussed?'

I tried to hide my shaking. 'He can't know it's me.'

Clambering out of the car, my limbs took double effort to control. Ms Fish opened the boot and shone a torch into Syd's face.

He hid beneath his hands, curled up like he was hiding from the Bogeyman.

'Don't speak!' Ms Fish bawled.

Syd simply quivered.

'Get out. *Now.*'

He looked smashed, like when we shared a joint behind the boiler room at school and I puked all over him. As he struggled up, I saw a lump on his forehead the size of an egg – and an egg with a double yolk at that. He dropped onto the tarmac.

'Get up.'

Syd obeyed, wobbly on his feet. 'I can't see!'

I pressed his glasses into his hand, cracked and probably useless. Ms Fish pulled out the gun, making sure he had a good view.

He fell down again.

'I said get *up.*' She dragged Syd to his feet, marching him at gunpoint.

I illuminated the way, my shaky hand giving the torch a flickering effect. Through the fence, stumbling over the tracks, we stopped in front of a set of buffers that – if it wasn't so dark – probably still had my blood on them.

'Turn around.' Ms Fish pointed the gun to his head. 'Sit.'

Syd simply dropped in the middle of the track. As I shone the torch over him, his eyes showed an emptiness, as though fear, bewilderment and a pistol whip had rendered him a vegetative state.

But shit happens, right? I'm just here trying to deal with it the best I can.

'So, Syd,' said Ms Fish with a 'so we meet again Mr Bond' kind of voice.

If she was expecting a reply, she didn't get one.

'I think you know why you're here?' She moved closer and pointed the gun at his groin. 'What have you got to say for yourself?'

Poor bastard – in his eyes it's going to be death by woman scorned. If he knew the real reason he'd probably perk up a bit – gangland treachery is definitely him. Daft sod.

'I can't hear you,' shouted Ms Fish.

There was some kind of whimper that perhaps resembled the word 'sorry'.

'Good.' She raised the gun to his head again. 'But don't get comfortable – we're not finished.' Ms Fish's tone rendered such a nastiness, I could only imagine the inspiration for which lay somewhere within her own personal scorn. 'The sight of you makes me sick. Do you know that? I want to puke just at the thought of you – and how you've... dishonoured me. I never want to have to see your ugly face again. What you going to do about that?'

He was quiet. Maybe he was thinking about it.

'I'll tell you what you're going to do. You're going to pack a bag and piss off far away from here. You're leaving this city and you're never coming back. Got it? And don't think I won't hunt you down if you disobey – only then I'll be scraping you from my boot—'

I coughed, waving downwards. Ms Fish slapped Syd on the back of the head. I intensified the hand gesture, shaking my head to boot, though this intensified the misinterpretation and, indeed, the slaps. Syd absorbed the punishment, releasing sporadic grunts, somewhere amongst which I could decipher the words: 'I know this is just front.'

Shit. You do?

'I know y're workin' for Chas.' Syd's voice became more desperate. 'But *I* dunno what 'appened at marina. I did everythin' he told me – I just fell asleep. Then I shit meself, knew it looked bad, I knew Chas'd be full a beef.' As the slapping had stopped, Syd spoke more quickly, seeming to make a correlation between the noise from his mouth and an absence of pain. 'So I sent the ring to Ginger – Ginger Jones. I dunno why, I was shittin' it, just wannid rid.'

Ms Fish was watching him intently, her big blue eyes glowing through her mask, almost brighter than the torch. 'Tell more about the ring,' she said.

No! Don't do that! She's a felon. Don't be fooled by those amazing tits.

'Like I say, Ginger Jones's got it now. But Chas knows, cos it's all in the letter I sent 'im.'

Letter? Why do my legs feel funny? Am I having a stroke?

Ms Fish gave Syd a swift, single slap. 'What did the letter say?'

Ok, clench buttocks, retract stool. No fear!

'Stop! It's me,' I blurted. I took off my mask and knelt by Syd. 'It's Ginger.'

'Just a minute, buster.' Ms Fish pointed the gun at me, waggling accusingly. 'What the hell is this? Don't think I've come here to play some stupid—'

'*Leave it.*' I prodded Syd. 'Can you hear me?'

He smiled slightly, mumbling, though remained in a heap; his voice was gentle, like he'd suffered a bereavement – or a smack round the head. 'S'ppose I 'ad it comin'.'

Suppose you did – but that's not the point anymore. 'You're right, you're here because of Chas,' I said. 'He's sure it was you who grassed him – asked me to sort it. I've been eating myself from the inside out thinking about this, how to "sort it". Bottom line is Syd, you've got to get away from here, a long way away, cos… Well, Chas'll kill you.'

His eyes opened wider and he winced in the torch-light. 'I 'an't done nowt,' he whispered.

Of course he hadn't – I knew that better than anyone. 'Whatever. You've just got to disappear – *anywhere*.'

'Y're working for him?'

'No… I… well… It just kinda happened.'

'So y'got the ring?'

I nodded, then glancing away to take a deep, shaky breath. 'What was that about writing a letter? To Chas?'

Syd groaned, rubbing the lump on his head. 'Just t'clear the air like and get things straight.'

'How long ago?'

'Dunno, few days after I s'ppose…'

You idiot!

'But I daren't send it – ummed and ahhed for yonks cos I thought it could do more bad than good – was doin' me 'ed in.'

'Did you send it?' I snapped.

'Yesterd'y – finally plucked the guts. Was a weight off me mind – felt loads better after.'

'So he'll only've got that today, right?'

'Dunno.'

Idiot. Maybe I should kill you.

'Soz for the ring thing,' Syd mumbled. 'Just wanted to get rid. There's too much history.'

Inside my head, I heard a laugh that was laced with sarcasm. *And I've gone and done the same thing to Brian. What a dickhead...* 'Hang on, what do you mean "history"?' I said. 'It belongs to his "ma"? Right?'

He seemed to shrink into himself a little. 'So y'*don't* know?'

Ms Fish grabbed Syd by his fancy Fred Perry shirt, pressing the gun into his forehead. 'So tell him.'

'OK! Chill!'

She backed off, just a little.

There was a long pause, God knows what he was thinking, how he gathered his thoughts to speak. But he did speak, if a little incoherently: 'It was a robbery – upper class, y'know, toffs and that. Some Lord-a-the-Manor was done for the family jewels. A gang done their 'omework and drove a big JCB into the estate, just rammed straight in and got away with a fortune – to pass on to dodgy collectors like. Tit bits filtered out 'ere and there, robber to robber like, stuff that was easier to get rid of – that's where Chas comes in.'

'His "*ma's*" ring?'

'Yeh. They say he got it off one a them robbers for "services rendered" – 'undred grand's worth!'

What?

'But who knows what's the truth with fellas like 'im,' said Syd. 'I'm just sayin' what I've 'eard.'

Bloody hell. I almost took fifty quid for it!

Ms Fish made herself known with a condescending sniff. 'So where is this ring?'

Syd sat up a little, rubbed his head. 'Y'got a bird?'

'No,' I said shortly.

He strained to focus on her. 'Nice tits, shame 'bout the mask.'

'Fuck off.' She pointed the gun at me, more accusingly than in threat. 'Where's the ring?'

'It's safe.'

She moved closer. 'Don't play me for a fool.'

'Are you daft? I *know* that's not real.'

'Now so does *he*.'

I waved her away dismissively. 'It doesn't matter – we're taking him back.'

'*No*.' Ms Fish actually stomped her foot. 'I want to know what this is all about.'

'I can't tell you that.'

'Fine then I'll rat on you.' She held out her arms and shouted into the darkness. 'Hello everybody! Ginger Jones has a stolen ring in his possession.'

I grabbed her arm, pulling her down and speaking through grinding teeth. 'You ever repeat that and I'll—'

'You'll what?'

'Just remember I know what *you've* done too.'

She was quiet, utterly.

'Who *is* she?' said Syd.

'A casual acquaintance – we're not friends or anything.'

Ms Fish swore under her breath, and then we took Syd home.

Twenty-Four

And when you flinch at a bump
in the night, think of my face…

Back at my place, Ms Fish and I took rest.

'So,' she said, mooching about the bedsit, furrowed brow communicating her distaste. 'What exactly *did* happen between you and Syd? And who's Chas?'

I flopped back on my bed, releasing just a little tension – I felt so close to getting all this sorted, close enough to smell the cigar, close enough to think that maybe life could be good after all. 'Sorry and all that, but I still don't trust you.'

Ms Fish looked away. 'Cut the tough guy crap – it doesn't suit you.'

We'd left Syd packing a suitcase, soon to be on route to wherever he'd end up. His acquiescence had seemed childlike, an avoidance of the monster that lived under his bed.

There was a bang on the door.

'Get that, will you?' I mumbled.

'At one-thirty in the morning? Get it yourself.'

The banging became more urgent, like someone had been told true happiness lay on the other side – I reckoned they'd be disappointed.

It was Syd.

He barged past. 'Ginger!'

Yes, that's my name.

'The Slap's out,' he blurted, grabbing me by the shoulders.

'What?'

'Got bailed. 'e's been seen.'

'But—'

''e's out!'

'He can't be let out before...'

Syd shook me, like he was trying to get the final grains from a salt cellar. ''e's out! I 'ad to warn ye.' Flapping his arms, he almost knocked off his glasses. ''e's been down Arthur's Shop, Pork Café, The Lion, *everywhere.* 'e's gonna kill me.'

I took a deep breath and gathered my thoughts.

'Ginger!'

'OK!' *Bloody hell, gimme time to think man...* 'Right...' *Shit! What do I say? The Slap's out... The Slap's out!* 'Just... er, calm down...' *Good one – that'll make everything OK.*

Syd's eyes were darting around the bedsit, as though death hid behind the curtains, or beneath the bed. 'What we gonna do?'

'Listen,' I said, followed by a shaky breath. 'As far as anyone knows, I've already "sorted you". Right? So all you've gotta do is disappear.'

Syd straightened his glasses, the crack across the lens like a mini fork of lightning. He appeared to think for a second, though his wide eyes looked far from pacified. 'But—'

'*Don't* make this any more complicated than it needs to be.' *This is complicated. This is deep. This is... just awful.* 'Stick to what we said.'

''e'll be comin' for y'too – for the ring.'

Indeed, my heart had been beating furiously since he'd mentioned the name. But I stayed calm, because the answer was simple. 'Then I'll just give it to him,' I said. *That is, via a desperate, panic-stricken call to Brian.*

Syd's hands were tremulous. 'Yeh... Course.'

We loitered for a moment, awkward body movements suggesting that inwardly, neither of us were convinced.

'Y'reckon we're all right then?' said Syd, a while later.

No. 'Yes.'

'Really?'

Don't make me say it again.

Syd's mobile rang. 'Syd?... 'ello Darl... What?... I'm at Ginger's... ten minutes... see y'soon.' He tucked the phone back into his pocket, his fingers still showing a tremor. 'I'm pickin' up yer Mary then we're off together... dunno where yet.'

'You *and* Mary?' I said.

'Yeh.'

'How you getting away?'

'An old Sierra, mate of a mate.'

It was quiet.

'Listen Ginger – gotta get goin'.'

I nodded. 'So... I'll see you then.'

'Yeh.'

Our eyes held for a moment.

He left.

'So who's "The Slap"?' said Ms Fish, straightening herself up.

'Just an old friend,' I mumbled.

She sniffed and tied her hair back. 'It's time I went too. I did as we agreed – so we're even. Right?'

God, she's pretty. I nodded. 'Thanks,' I said.

'I'd say see you around, but I don't want to see you ever again.'

'If that's what you want.'

'It is.'

My eyes followed as she proceeded with a conspicuous exit, opening the door with an exaggerated sway to her hips. She glanced back, though offered no detectable hint of affection. I smiled to myself, content with the consolation of a fleeting blowjob. Ms Fish turned to leave.

And screamed.

The Slap shoved Syd into the room, slamming the door as though it had called his mother a whore. He held a gun.

Ms Fish was down on the floor, hands over her ears and eyes clenched shut. The Slap pointed his gun, gesturing for me to join her. I obliged and we huddled together. Syd stood with arms folded across his chest, his back against the wall. He whispered in tongues, I think to God – funny that.

The Slap kept us static under his weapon, reaching into his trench coat to produce a mobile phone. He dialled singlehandedly, an intensity that should have pushed his thumb through the casing.

This is all just a misunderstanding, right? He's calling the pizza dude.

He threw the phone across to me, giving a short nod, I grasped it with jelly hands.

'*Speak,*' said the phone.

'W-who is this?' I said.

'You need to ask?'

Indeed. I wasn't stupid – the 'got a brick stuck in my throat' voice could have belonged to no-one else.

'C-Chas?'

'Give the kid a biscuit.'

What can I say? The game's up.

I could hear his teeth grinding: 'So what I'm asking myself – sitting here a guest of Her Majesty – is "why has Syd packed his suitcase and trotted off to see Ginger?"'

I took strength from Ms Fish's embrace. I felt a tremble to her hand, I felt her heart beat, her breaths become quicker; to know that such a conniving, confident woman could be as equally scared, it was soothing.

'I-I don't know,' I blurted.

'I must be psychic – cos I knew you were gonna say that.'

I glanced up at The Slap, standing over the room like Colossus Of Bedsits, his battered trench coat packed with muscle – muscle you didn't mess with.

'Where is it?' said Chas.

The ring!

'It's safe. I promise.' I tried to be brave, but was as convincing as custard of the cowardly kind.

'Tell me, you like it?'

I paused.

'Nice and shiny? Worth a few quid you reckon?'

'I… dunno.'

'Really?'

'Just a ring…'

His voice became a growl, like conversing with a lawnmower. 'Has someone been telling you tales?'

'No. Well, I've heard… like, rumours I suppose.'

'And what rumours might they be?'

'Like you said – it might be worth a few quid.'

'That why you and Syd are doing a runner?'

'What?'

'You heard me.'

'No.'

'Some other reason then?'

'No! I mean, we're not. I'm sorting it.'

'I put trust in you.'

My voice became more desperate, as it seemed did any chance of this ending with a handshake. 'I'm *sorting* it.'

'Big temptation for a young kid – if he's got the bollocks to think he can get away with it.'

'You've got it wrong…'

'I know you've got bollocks – you just don't know how to use 'em. Shame really – that it has to end like this.'

'Listen—'

'Shut up.'

I did.

'Get it. Now.'

'I can't. I mean, I *can*. Just not, er…' The power of articulation was absorbed by the turmoil that was my tummy.

Chas's growl became a few semitones higher. 'Don't play me for a fucking clown.'

'An hour. I just need an hour.'

'You've got thirty seconds until everyone in that room goes bye bye.'

'It's with a friend!' I blurted.

'Who?'

'I can't—'

'*Who?*'

Fuck! 'Brian Scrimshaw!'

'Now tell me where he is.'

'At home, probably. But I can call him.'

'How far?'

'Goddard Ave, I think, I'm not exactly sure.'

There was a heavy breath, like whenever Dad received a council tax demand, then a pause. 'Give the phone back.'

The Slap pounced on my sudden movement and I found myself staring down the barrel of a gun – I just knew he'd have no compunction.

'He wants to talk to *you*,' I yelped, clenching my eyes shut, holding the phone at arm's length. 'Take it.' There was a strong tug, I let go and snatched my arm back – Ms Fish and I then squeezing to the point of pain.

'Let *me* talk to 'im,' said Syd, voice a feeble displacement of air. 'I wanna tell it straight. Tell him I'm no grass.'

Stop talking Syd, eh? This isn't a 'Tell The Truth Anonymously' meeting.

I opened my eyes, Syd back against the wall, shivering inside his own cuddle. 'Just calm it,' I said, a tremor to my own tone suggesting do what I say not what I do. 'Keep it together and keep quiet. We'll be fine.' There wasn't a shred of bravery to the words, just a fear of the truth, my own comeuppance.

Syd obeyed, probably by panic induced mind freeze. The Slap took a step forward, pointing his gun closer to our faces, reasserting his control. He held the phone with his opposite hand, gesturing for me to take it.

'You listening?' said Chas.

I swallowed, audibly. 'Yeh,' I mumbled.

'You're gonna phone your "friend". Got it?'

'Yeh.'

'You put it on speaker, loud – so everyone can hear. Got it?'

'Yeh.'

'Use your own phone, so he knows the number. Be nice and be *quick* – any funny shit and it's bye bye Ginger. Right? You getting this?'

'Yeh.'

'Good. Do it.'

'Right, er...' As I made to pass back the phone, my jelly hands lost grip, it bounced several times over the carpet, hit The Slap's boot – a thud suggested steel toecaps. 'I'm sorry.'

Betraying no more emotion than a car park, The Slap kept eye contact as he scooped up the phone, grunting to the master.

'I... I need *my* phone,' I said. 'To call Brian. I'm supposed to call Brian.'

Upon a brown cardboard box/bedside table sat the mobile phone I'd loaned from Ms Fish. The Slap strode sideways, his gait taking in half the room, hand like a claw grasping a cuddly toy as he took my phone, a stride back to place it into my hand.

'S-so? I just call him?' I said. *No. Stick it up your arse and deposit it to the second shelf. Idiot.*

The Slap nodded, his gun dipping slightly and appearing to nod with him. Having established the bleeding obvious, I loosened my embrace with Ms Fish, fingers limp as I tried to operate the phone. I cranked the volume, numerous prods and pokes elicited a ringing tone loud enough for the room to hear; at which point, like rancid socks, I held the phone at arm's length. The Slap held Chas's call aloft, Brian picked up, and so began a conference call that was as much intimidating as it was technologically inept.

'Brian. It's me,' I said brightly – the pointing gun made the creation of such a fake tone rather painstaking.

'Ginger? What the hell? What's wrong?' His reply was brash, suggesting he'd been awoken and was none too thankful for the trouble.

'Nothing,' I chirped.

'Pardon? What do you mean?'

'I just wanted to, er, you know...' A flash of reality and the hopelessness of such scrambled my thinking.

Brian snapped: 'Ginger, *why* are you calling me?'

'I, well...' I took a long, deep breath. 'I just thought you might wanna come round?'

'Really? Why would I want to do that?' His petulance felt like a kick in the stomach.

'I need to see you,' I said.

'It's stupid o'clock, Ginger!'

'I *need* to see you. Right now.'

'Oh.' I heard him gulp, the deeper tone with which he continued suggesting an enormous misinterpretation. 'Well, why didn't you just say?'

With no thoughts more cunning, I chose to not set him straight. 'I, er, didn't know how,' I said quickly.

'But it's so sudden.'

'These things happen.'

'I never really thought—'

'Brian, just get here. And bring that ring.'

'Pardon? Why?'

161

I paused, then cringing as I said: 'Dressing-up.'

'Oh, Ginger!'

I ended the call.

Back in the room, I wondered if it would just be easier to get shot. The Slap was still threatening as such, and the reasons of resistance were headed the same way as reasons to be cheerful.

'Very good,' said Chas. His voice reminded me of a late night jazz DJ growling from a car radio.

'Brian's probably twenty minutes away,' I said, timidly.

Chas gave a grunt, a moment's quietness affording me a glance to Ms Fish, then to Syd, both clearly petrified, and with my own shaky bones alongside, The Slap loomed over us like a guilty secret and the fear of retribution.

Then Chas said: 'We wait.'

Twenty-Five

Grasp with both hands
what life may have to hold.

The red LEDs of my alarm clock showed that fourteen minutes had passed between Chas ending the call and a gentle rapping from out in the hall – it seemed Brian was six minutes keener than I'd anticipated.

The Slap settled his eyes over me, his impatient gun waggle an instruction to answer the door. I separated myself from Ms Fish and followed his command, pulling down on the latch with snail paced preciseness.

'Ginger?' The voice was soft, inquisitive, arriving in advance of the door reaching full gape. 'Ginger?' Brian stood opposed, framed by the door jamb – he raised a carefully tweezed eyebrow. 'I can't believe that you… I mean, after all this time, in the office…'

'I'm sorry—'

His gaze had drifted over my shoulder, the high frequency of the following yelp confirmation he had clocked The Slap. 'Ginger!'

I looked back, ducking instinctively as The Slap took aim. 'No. Please.' My arms stretched out like a birdman, I straightened up to form a human shield. 'Brian's not a part of this, he's just—'

Behind me, I heard a thud, then performing a kind of lopsided pirouette that was almost tragic in its lack of grace, I saw Brian in the hall, sprawled over the linoleum, his spiky hair reminiscent of hedgehog road kill.

Oh God!

I crouched, substituting my lack of first aid knowledge with panic-stricken prods. Several moments of prodding brought me to realise that if Brian had taken a bullet, said bullet must have passed through *me*, and *I* felt fine – notwithstanding The Slap's gun, the hostage situation and my general dissatisfaction with life, that is. No, I was sure no shot had been fired. Indeed, Brian was breathing – it appeared he'd fainted.

Thank you God. Really, thank you.

I looked back to The Slap, his gaze vacant, distributing gun points between the hall and the bedsit. He offered several gestures via his weapon, I seized the meanings: 'Close the fucking door!' and 'Drag the gay into the bedsit.' So I did.

I flipped Brian onto his back, laying him beside my bed, delicately so. Kneeling over him, I found it hard to comprehend the fuck-up I was making of everyone's lives – though I did appear to be very good at it.

The Slap handed me his phone, wide eyes darting from one hostage to another.

'Everyone sitting comfortably?' said Chas.

I took a deep breath. 'Yeh.'

He growled: 'Better get what's mine.'

My fear had become a predictable response to Chas's voice, it compelled my jelly fingers to probe the bulge over Brian's pocket. His jeans were tight, a fraction of an inch from a compression fracture, and even though his cock appeared as an entirely separate bulge, I couldn't help but cringe as three of my digits entered the denim. My fumbling was swift, I withdrew pinching a drawstring pouch.

'Take it,' I blurted. The pouch was of a purple velvet, I held it at arm's length. 'The ring's in there.' *Well, I hope it is. Please don't let it be a condom or flavoured body paint or a vibrating cock ring.*

The Slap scowled as I plonked said pouch into his digger hand. Using his teeth to tear the velvet, he spat the remnants with such force that a spray of spittle struck my forehead, feeling like a hail shower. The veins of his temple inflated, he concentrated over the ring, then tucking it away inside his trench coat, he tossed me back to Ms Fish as though flicking something from his finger.

I brought the phone to my ear. 'H-he's got it,' I said.

There was a pause, Chas took a long breath. 'That's very good.'

'So… I mean… what happens now?'

He laughed. 'Bye Ginger.'

The line went dead.

I kind of got the feeling we were all heading in that general direction. I looked at The Slap, like a statue, expressionless, four dickheads at the point of his gun. The pose held, for what seemed like a fortnight, ample time to contemplate one's death.

Syd stepped forward, arms outstretched, like The Angel of the North. 'Listen. Y'gotta 'ear me out.' His voice rendered a kind of breathless delirium. 'I dunno what Chas's told ye, but it weren't me!'

The Slap was still.

'I'm no grass, 'onest I aint.'

Be quiet Syd, for God's sake.

Ms Fish and I scrambled across the floor, huddling into a corner. Brian stirred, groaning as he struggled to sit upright.

'Just listen,' said Syd, mixing his words with spittle.

It was quiet for a moment.

Boom.

The Slap shot him.

The noise was painful. I squeezed my eyes shut, clutched at Ms Fish. Syd was dead. I didn't need to look – it fell so silent. The stillness sustained, goading. As I dared to peek, I saw The Slap settle his gun over us both. I'd never been more certain of anything in my life.

We were going to die.

Twenty-Six

You're lipstick is red,
Sydney is dead.

It's kind of strange – knowing that you have seconds to live. It's not much time to fit in all the things you've been meaning to get round to – a haircut, a new pair of pants, a girlfriend – the list went on; though time, it appeared, would not.

Ms Fish clenched her eyes, shivering. I thought I should say something, but I was quiet, frozen by a pointed gun. There was a yelp, I glanced to see Brian sit up, vomit and then pass out again – it seemed he'd eaten carrots recently.

Meanwhile, the moment was close, The Slap's finger jittered against the trigger.

Go to sleep my baby.

Close your pretty eyes...

Am I dead? I don't feel dead. But then how would I know? I've never been dead before. Everything feels in order...

I opened my eyes.

I saw a gun.

I shut them again.

The whole thing was taking a lot longer than I'd anticipated. *Still, perhaps one shouldn't hurry death... No. It's definitely taking too long.*

I opened my eyes once more, grasping courage to keep them that way. The Slap remained, as did the gun at the end of his arm – his face void of expression, like a snooker ball.

But I'm alive!

He reached out, tugged the sheets from my bed, dropping them over Syd. As the sheets settled, so Syd's blood was drawn into the fibres. A gun waggle summoned us to rise, Ms Fish and I standing together.

'Wrap him,' said The Slap. His voice was shit-making. I mean, he sounded bored, like he was the talking clock and he'd said the same 'the time is now' fifty thousand times that day – there was no emotion. I much preferred the mute.

I did as I was told, looking at the ceiling, down at the bare bed, anything but at what my hands were doing. Syd was warm, like he was just sleeping – but people don't spill pints of blood when they're sleeping.

Then I caught sight of Brian, he *was* sleeping, kind of. Slumped beside my bed, his face had retained its fear and looked like a Halloween mask – it made me think there were too many bodies strewn over my bedsit floor. Ms Fish whimpered, and I looked up as The Slap took aim.

'No!' My voice was a roar and seemed to be functioning of its own accord, damned if it was going to let another friend die. 'He's not a witness – he's barely spent five seconds conscious! Leave him. Please, just leave him.'

The Slap lowered his gun, though perhaps he had already decided to do so. I reckoned a second murder had only been postponed, equal three way betting on which one of us would be next. He took a hold of Ms Fish, quenching a yelp as he closed his big digger hand over her face.

'Outside. Take him,' he said.

I screwed up my face, took hold of Syd's dirty trainers and dragged him across the floor. Out in the hall I could hear screams as the woman next door pleasured a client – it covered the thud as Syd's head struck the doorstep. Blood smeared the floor like some kind of hellish slug trail. The Slap followed after me, Ms Fish a puppet to his gun. The Sierra had been parked hurriedly across the footpath, and as I dropped Syd beside, the noise rebounded through the stillness. It would have been blatant to any early-morning curtain twitcher, and I clung to the hope that someone might send the police to rescue us.

Seduced by The Slap's gun, I picked up Syd's skin and bone and spilled him into the boot – retching as his blood smeared my T-shirt.

'Drive,' said The Slap.

'I-I can't.'

'*Drive.*'

'I don't know how!'

Ms Fish spoke through a gasp. '*I* can drive.'

He paused, then shoved her to me. 'Get in.'

We obeyed the gun.

Inside smelt of vanilla, and the seats were real leather. Ms Fish clipped her seat belt into place, her tremulous hand brushed back and she lifted her top a little. Tucked into her waistline I saw our own spud gun. 'Put on your seat belt,' she mumbled.

I did.

The Slap folded himself to fit the back seat, gun moving rhythmically between our heads. 'Drive,' he said.

Ms Fish grasped the steering wheel tight, though her hands were still shaking. 'Where?'

'*Drive.*'

We took off, in no particular direction, though I reckoned our final destination would be just that. I clung to my seat for dear life.

Ms Fish's eyes were wide, I think a little recklessness had mixed with the fear, but hey, if we were going to die anyway…

The empty streets reverberated, tyres squealing like they'd just caught their husbands' in bed with a floozy. Such speed would have made me nervous, had I not a gun in the back of my head.

'Snuff Mill,' said The Slap.

I screwed up my face – I didn't think we were going there for a picnic.

We got faster.

God. I'm going to die…

I snatched the gun from Ms Fish, pointing back to The Slap.

Still we got faster.

'I'll fucking shoot you.' The words scraped along my throat like a string of barbed wire – I sounded more likely to cry than to commit murder.

The Slap was still, pointing, not a twitch to betray his thinking.

We stared at one another.

'Think of your nan,' I blurted.

He stared.

'I saw you – inside. You were crying. What if she could see you now?'

The car swerved.

There was a shot.

The windscreen shattered.

Ms Fish screamed.

Another shot.

Imagine being packed into a box and thrown down a long flight of stairs – that's what it felt like. Ms Fish hugged the steering wheel, seeming to think she had control as the car sprawled over the street. A row of parked cars appeared, an imminent destination.

Ms Fish glanced at me.

The cars came closer.

She accelerated.

I closed my eyes.

I can't remember a great deal of what happened then. The sound of dry, clashing metal, the notion of being in a washing machine during a spin cycle – and then the world cut out.

My eyes opened a while later, or so I assume – unconsciousness is a long way from the nearest clock. My head hurt, I knew that.

'Ginger? Ginger!'

The front of the car was mangled – and spread over the bonnet, like he'd been cut from a butcher's hook, was The Slap.

I heard a voice. 'Are you OK?'

I took a moment to focus on Ms Fish. She was bloody, but smirked at me.

'Are you OK!'

I held my head and shrugged.

Ms Fish wiped an oozing laceration to her forehead, glancing to the lump of meat in front of us. 'No seat belt you see.'

'I think he's breathing.'

She shrugged.

I unstrapped myself and kicked open the side door. My legs felt like dangly string and I dropped to my knees – Ms Fish tried to help, but I just lay in the road.

She held a tissue over her wound and brushed her blood-mingled hair behind her ear. 'Is anything broken?'

'My head hurts,' I mumbled.

'Someone should look at that.'

No shit.

She sat with me.

My head ached for a thousand Anadin – I wanted to be safe, snuggled in the fortress of my own bed. I couldn't grasp what had happened to me, it was like trying to pick out a whisper from the opposite side of a packed football ground. There was so much noise in my head but it was gibberish. I gave up and tried to cry, but my eyes were dry and stingy.

It was quiet.

'I don't know what to say,' said Ms Fish.

'No?'

She smiled a little. 'We could be friends, almost.'

'Almost?'

'Different people, different worlds.'

'And one big collision.'

'Yes, very big.'

Fuck, my head hurts.

'I think the police'll be quite interested,' she said.

My voice sounded more desperate than I'd have liked. 'But what shall we *tell* the police?'

She crossed her lips with a finger. I struggled to look up at the carnage – it would have taken a big rug to sweep under all that shit.

We sat together, bloody, but I was glad to be alive, to have someone sat beside me. I just had nothing left – not strength, nor fight nor thought.

I beheld my partner in crime. Her pretty, bloody face showed a wide stare, sporadic blinks seeming to take snapshots of the mess we'd created. She stirred a little and looked back at me – as if she remembered she'd left the iron on.

'Ginger?'

I looked as attentive as I was capable.

'What about that ring?'

As I peered back, a hallucination framed her eyes in the ring's outline. 'Don't,' I muttered.

She appeared to hesitate, presumably initiating the weird thought processes that made her *her.*

I closed my eyes. 'Just don't.'

'But…'

I lay back over the road and drifted off.

'Ginger…?'

When I opened my eyes, I reckoned Ms Fish would be gone.

Twenty-Seven

Diamonds and pearls
could sustain this girl.

My world had been still for a while. During that while I had lost myself in a lovely quietness, simply drifting. Now, that quietness was rescinding. I could make out hurried footsteps somewhere close. I heard voices too, reverberating, without clarity, like I had water in my ears. My eyes felt so heavy.

'What's the matter with him?'

'We're not sure.'

'Will he be all right?'

'You'll have to wait outside.'

My eyes were opened forcibly and a piercing light felt like a laser on my retina. I was lying down, I could see ceiling tiles and two strip-lights glowing.

'Ginger? Can you hear me?'

'What?' I mumbled.

'You've been in an accident.'

You reckon?

'You're in the Hull Royal Infirmary.'

'But...'

'Do you know what day it is?'

I was quiet. The pain in my head was an acute throb and I felt sick. *Hospital eh? This must be one hell of a hangover.* A nurse in scrubs peered over me.

'Can you tell me your address Ginger? Do you know where you live?' she said.

Of course I know where I live, miss.

'No? What about your date of birth?'

Yes. 'Er...'

'OK. Don't worry.'

I'm not.

'Can you look forward for me Ginger?' She shone the light into each eye again.

'OK. How do you feel Ginger? Any pain?'

'My head hurts.'

'Where exactly?'

'Inside.'

'Can you describe the pain?'

'I feel...' I lurched downwards and was sick on her shoes. She handed me a bowl which I spat into.

'Sorry.'

Across the room a commotion caught my attention. A trolley burst through double doors, the man upon it strapped to a spinal board, the neck brace and ventilation would have otherwise provided a disguise, had the man not been colossal – The Slap sure looked peaky.

My mind was beginning to operate with more clarity. It wasn't that I'd forgotten, I think I'd just chosen not to recall. As I watched the fuss around The Slap, I wondered why I'd ended up in resus.

'OK Ginger,' said the nurse – she was dark and pretty, 'we need to take you down for a CT to make sure there's nothing going on inside your head that we don't know about.'

Well, she doesn't know I'm imagining the colour of her bra for a start.

I was wheeled out into a corridor.

'Ginger?' Ms Fish halted the trolley. Her familiar face was welcome to me – the cut on her forehead had been tidied with Steri-Strips. 'What's happening?'

The auxiliary moving me answered: 'He has a slightly low GCS and needs a CT.'

'What the hell is that supposed to mean?' Ms Fish blurted.

'We just need to make sure all's well in Ginger's head.'

We carried on down the corridor, Ms Fish walked alongside the trolley.

'How did I get here?' I said.

'You went a little strange,' said Ms Fish.

'What?'

'Then passed out.'

'Right.'

'It seemed rather hairy for a moment.'

'Suppose that fills in the gap.' I didn't feel as bad as her look of concern should suggest. '*You* OK?' I asked.

'Fine.' She touched her wound tentatively, pulling a face. 'If a little sore.'

I flinched, trying to dispel a blood-laced flashback. 'What happened to Brian?'

'They said he needed observation – not that it's any of *my* business. They thought we were all together.'

We are!

As we moved along the corridor, the auxiliary flashed us a perfunctory smile. Ms Fish returned her distaste with a short sniff, then shielded her mouth and whispered like a bitchy schoolgirl. 'So… what happens now Ginger?'

'Brain scan, right?'

'No, I should say, what do we…'

'Eh?'

'... *say?*'

'What?'

'We're stuck here, who knows for how long.'

'Well yeh, it looks like it.'

'And people might be enquiring. They'll want to know the full story – *everything.*'

'Probably.'

'We should work something out, tell everyone the same thing.'

'Like the truth?'

She paused. 'Perhaps a close derivative.'

'For God's sake...'

'There could be repercussions.'

'What you talking about? *We* did nothing wrong.'

'We gave Syd quite a tough time, there's Daddy's money, and...'

'I've got a headache!'

'People might be looking for that ring.'

'Let them look – it's not our problem.'

We stopped before some double doors, Ms Fish glanced away.

'*Is it* our problem?' I asked.

She didn't reply.

Fuck.

The auxiliary gestured Ms Fish to a side and pushed me through the doors. 'You'll have to stay outside, miss.'

'I'll wait for you Ginger,' said Ms Fish after me.

Indeed, but will the torment?

Inside, I was transferred to an examination table, positioned by a technician and given a brief explanation of the procedure. Then, my head was moved back into the centre of what I can only describe as a giant Polo mint, which then buzzed and whirred for a few minutes.

Syd is dead! Oh God! My friend. My enemy. It's my fault.

I imagined the machine was cooking my brain, from the centre outwards – I wanted it to erase the feelings of helplessness, of guilt, to just erase my whole mind!

'All done,' said a voice.

Back on the trolley, and into the corridor, I ignored the auxiliary's polite conversation over her new diet and the healthy bacteria in her breakfast drink. Anyway, she was promptly muted as two familiar faces ambushed us.

'We wanna talk to him,' said one.

'Police,' said the other.

Briggs and Johnson. Oh dear.

'You'll both have to wait,' said the auxiliary.

'*Now.*' Briggs's tash was rather bushier than I remembered and his voice came through like a poacher firing a gunshot from beneath a hedge.

'No.'

'Look here, miss…'

'We're going back to an assessment room and the doctor can decide if Ginger's able.'

Briggs hung at one side of the trolley as the auxiliary pushed us on, lanky Johnson taking the other flank, his limbs lacking any grace as he struggled to keep pace.

'He looks all right to me,' said Briggs. He frowned and both their faces moved in, peering as though I were an exceptionally ugly baby wrapped up in a cot.

'Where's the lass Ginger?' said Briggs 'They said she'd come with you?'

I closed my eyes and was quiet. *When she saw you mate – I reckon she's long gone.*

'Do you know how serious this is?'

Well, quite.

'One body, maybe another on the way…'

Don't remind me, please.

'I need some answers. I need names.'

Chas.

'*This* shit won't just disappear.'

Hell, I wish it would.

'We'll keep someone looking over you, make sure you're safe.'

Thanks.

'No sudden movements, and everything'll be all right.'

Can I hold you to that?

'Now just leave him alone,' said the auxiliary.

It went quiet for a few moments, so I guessed they had.

'Sounds like a mess,' said the auxiliary, much more gently.

I felt safe with my eyes closed. 'Yes, it is.'

'Well let's just hope that scan comes back as normal.'

I thought for a moment. 'Suppose.'

'That's it – fighting talk.'

My mind drifted from her voice. I'd had enough of fighting; and as for the scan – to be honest, I didn't really care.

Twenty-Eight

I guess I'm not
what you want.

The local hospital was a looming grey relic from the 1960s. A hodgepodge of concrete fourteen floors high, I found myself peering from a window on the tenth. Such a vantage point offered an expansive view of the city – far reaching into the horizon, cars and buses weaving between hundreds of years' worth of redevelopment after redevelopment, the houses and shops relics of their own particular decade, all having once been the future.

It was a bright, Sunday morning, and I'd been admitted for observation, though was being more closely observed by a policeman on the other side of the door. I was reckoning on a visit from Briggs and his bushy moustache any time soon, and quite what I was going to tell him was making my headache worse. I wanted Ms Fish to be with me – she could have told me what to do.

Such musing was infiltrated by voices coming from outside my room:

'No-one but immediate family and medical staff,' said the policeman.

'He's fifty-percent my sperm.'

'Pardon, sir?'

'Like I said.'

'Sorry, could you just clarify what you mean, sir?'

'What do you want me to say? Dad?'

To be honest, I didn't much like the sound of 'Dad' either. I mean, it was probable I now shared as much DNA with a fat bloke with sideburns who'd emptied the clinical waste – and at least *he* had amusing facial hair. I stared out of the window and up into the wide blue sky, hoping to draw some of the clarity to my own mind. I hoped Dad hadn't arrived to ask how I was doing, because that would mean the whole world really was spinning out of control. As such, it seemed to follow that to maintain an element of order I should speak to him, allowing him to make bad. I straightened my hospital gown and was sure to cover my bottom. Decisiveness was in short supply, though what vestige I could grasp I took with me across to the door and pulled it open.

'What do you want?' I said, my grip tremulous upon the door handle.

Dad appeared unmoved by the sight of his son in a hospital gown, *in* hospital. 'Well, it's visiting time innit?' he said, his tone rather indignant. 'I'm not here to look pretty.'

The policeman appeared to be weighing the two of us up, perhaps in pursuit of a family resemblance. 'So he's…?'

I nodded, though in hindsight a resigned shrug would have been more fitting. Dad gave a short, smug smirk and pushed past the policeman, entering my room with a lopsided walk. He looked as though he'd spent the night fully clothed in his bed, his polo shirt crumpled like one of his discarded betting slips, his grey comb-over wackily unkempt. I stood by the window, a crack along the back of my hospital gown warming my flesh in the sun.

'What the bloody hell's going on?' said Dad.

His regular derision annoyed me. 'Well, I'm not dead.'

'What?'

'Not that I've had much support for the cause, but thanks for asking.'

Dad huffed and puffed to sit on the edge of my bed, seeming to observe the cold, clinical décor with a little antipathy. 'Stop talking bollocks.'

I struggled for anything else to say. 'So… How was the break with Mum?'

'Cut short!'

Fuck you. 'OK, do you wanna just tell me *why* you're here?'

He held me with peering eyes, like those of a gerbil. 'Let some air in, eh?'

My hospital gown barely hid my bottom as I turned a ratchet and the window slid open from the top. 'So?'

Dad continued to peer, though the odd glance passed by and out through the window. 'A bloke collared me this morning,' he said. 'We'd just got back and I was off to café for my dinner – Mum went for a walk see and she'd left nowt in.'

'Make a sandwich?'

'What?' He continued: 'So this black cab pulls up and the driver shouts me over – rough lookin' bugger too.'

'So?'

Dad appeared very serious, his brow scrunched, like whenever he accidently dropped food onto the floor. 'You need to listen to me carefully, right?'

I did.

'Chas says you've disrespected him. He says you've got one last chance to give it back. That's all.'

I looked at him hard. *He means the ring right? But if he does, then Ms Fish has taken it. Fuck.* 'Give what back, exactly?'

'That bloody ring. Jesus! I don't know how the hell you've gotten into this mess – *again!*

The heat along my back radiated and I felt my face flush. I felt too moist to be comfortable. 'I...' *How the hell do I explain? It's all so convoluted it makes my head feel like ginger spaghetti.* I gave a protracted sigh. 'I don't know either,' I mumbled.

'Well you need to take *this*.' Dad handed me a crumpled scrap of paper, the scrawl upon it I presumed to be a telephone number. 'Get in touch.'

'Who's this number for?'

Dad threw his arms in the air. 'Well it's not "phone-a-fucking-friend" is it – cos you don't fucking have any.'

'So Chas?'

'I don't know. I don't bloody know. But don't involve me.'

I glared at him. 'He would have had me killed last night.'

Dad shrugged. 'You're *not* dead, you said it yourself.'

'The way I see it I tell the police exactly what happened and Chas never sees the light of day. Works for me.'

'So then he comes for me and Mum.'

'What?'

'That's what's gonna happen.'

'How do you know? He might—'

'He won't give up! Can you live with that hanging over you? Me and Mum shouldn't have to.'

'If he's locked up, yes.'

'Every day of the rest of your life? With that thought in the back of your mind. Until...'

'What?'

'You know, me and Mum have been together twenty years and I've not seen her cry since she ditched the dancing – for *you* – and she spilled bloody buckets when we heard about all... *this*. So get it sorted.' Dad struggled to stand, there being a kind of unsteady haphazardness to his steps that made his walk to the door vaguely entertaining.

'I could be in here for days,' I said.

'You're not dying.'

I grunted.

'But don't take *my* word for it,' said Dad.

My mind held on to what he'd said, using the words to create a predicament I could barely fathom. An image of Syd seeped into my mind, bleeding; The Slap, strewn over the bonnet; the ring, glimmering. I shook the visions away at once – deferring such thoughts seemed my only chance of coping. I gazed out of the window. It was a big city outside, somewhere inside of which was Ms Fish – and it seemed my life depended on finding her.

Twenty-Nine

I just wanna be alone now,
there's no-one, no place for me.

'Your dad?' said Briggs about ten minutes later. 'What did he want?'

'He's my dad!' I replied, upright in bed. 'He was worried.'

'The Muppet on the door thinks otherwise.'

'I've suffered a personal injury that wasn't my fault – where there's blame there's a claim. We were discussing solicitors.'

'Don't get cute sunbeam.'

Briggs and Johnson had arrived in a fluster, seemingly desperate to unravel a story. Of course, what they didn't realise was that the threads they were tugging dangled from a story yet to reach a conclusion, and I was as keen to know the ending.

'OK,' said Briggs, pulling over a chair, 'Talk!'

I gazed with wide – hopefully – innocent eyes, and as he sat at my bedside the chair creaked under the weight of his last four take-aways.

'I don't know what to say,' I said.

'We've got all the time in the world tucked away in this little room – so take a deep breath.'

Johnson loitered around the other side of my bed, sniffing occasionally, hands in pockets and dragging his feet for odd glances out of the window. I remembered my first encounter with these two policemen, back at the station, and the meekness exuded by Johnson – I reckoned he was more suited to the Boys' Brigade.

If Ms Fish were here now, she'd have me out of this interrogation in a flash – beautiful girls always seem to have extra powers of manipulation.

For my contingency plan, I could think only to employ a trick I'd learned from Dad: I screamed and grasped my head.

The policemen stared, seeming to judge my performance like sternly faced theatre critics.

So, I screamed again.

'What the hell's the matter with you?' said Briggs. 'Be quiet for God's sake!'

'Nurse!' I spluttered.

Briggs sucked air through his teeth, I think calculating the consequences of calling my bluff. 'How bad is it?'

'*Bad.*'

He glanced across the bed to Johnson and grumbled: 'Get someone in here.'

Johnson obeyed, summoning a nurse who was plump, midlife, and greying. 'What's all this noise?' she said.

Briggs nodded in my direction. 'Sort him out will you.'

'Headache?'

I'm not holding my knee, sweetheart. 'Yes, it hurts.'

Her tone was gentle. 'How long?'

'Since…' I looked at Briggs.

'You two give him some rest,' she said, frowning at the policemen in turn.

'Just give him a bloody pill. This is important!'

'You can come back in a few hours.'

The nurse held the door and gestured for the policemen to exit – though they were not quick to depart, prolonged eye contact making me think Briggs was building up to ask me out on a date. I considered blowing him a kiss, though realised his further antagonism wouldn't really be to my advantage. Indeed, before long it was just me and the nurse, the room feeling altogether more salubrious.

What time I had forged, I took to think.

PART FIVE

Two hours later

Thirty

*It has never been
and it will never be.*

My hospital gown was speckled white, front fitting and fastened via sporadic buttons along the back – I found constant difficulty in covering my bottom. Accordingly, as I ventured out onto the ward, I flashed the policeman guarding my room.

'Sir!' he said, as I mooched by. 'For your own protection, sir, you must stay in your room. And cover up.'

'Sorry.' I pulled the gown over my modesty. 'I need the toilet – I haven't been since... I've got tummy ache.'

The policeman didn't reply, fidgeting on his feet – so I smiled and carried on along the corridor. The communal washroom was a consequence of an outdated 1960s hospital, and housed showers, washbasins and toilets. Inside, an elderly gentleman was undressing.

'Afternoon,' he said.

I nodded.

'I'm going home today.' He stretched his arms, sporting y-fronts, a considerable girth and much grey body hair. 'Better look smart.'

If you say so mister.

The man moved rather creakily into one of the shower cubicles, his clothes folded and stacked by the washbasin – a pair of black-rimmed spectacles rested at the pinnacle.

Just like... Oh Syd!

As the old man hummed a tune, I stole his clothes, a brown shirt and beige breeches offering an elevated waistline that folded double beneath the belt. His loafers were a half a size too small, and I limped to peer out onto the ward.

Outside, the policeman had moved to stand over the washroom. He held a hushed conversation via his mobile, shooting glances up the corridor. I ducked back, my eyes then scanning the washroom and settling upon a red cuboid stuck to the wall:

FIRE

BREAK GLASS

→●←

PRESS HERE

Without hesitation, I pressed my thumb through the Perspex, and as commanded, the alarm sounded with a kind of intermittent chime. I hid inside a shower cubicle, spreading my body as I stood with my back against the door. Footsteps seemed to scurry in time to the alarm, I could hear voices, the repetition of 'stay where you are' and 'don't worry'.

'Mr Jones?'

Who's there?

'Mr Jones?'

The policeman's voice reverberated, the cold tiles of the washroom seeming to taint his tone with harshness. '*Mr Jones!*'

I was quiet to the extent of holding my breath. The policeman's heels hit the tiles with exaggerated force, easily distinguishable over the background of running water and restrained panic. A mist had expanded from the cubicle next door, the old man evidently enjoying a very hot shower, oblivious to the world outside.

The footsteps stopped. 'Mr Jones? Do you hear the alarm?'

I'm not deaf mate.

'Can you hear me?'

Like I said…

'Answer me Mr Jones. Before I force the door… Mr Jones?'

You're in serious danger of wearing out my name, mate.

'Stand back from the door, Mr Jones.'

There was a clatter.

Bang.

Wallop.

The noise brought little change to my surroundings, a nonplussed retake confirming my position – locked inside a shower cubicle, alone.

'Someone get in here!' The policeman's voice cracked and rose an octave, complementing the air of urgency provoked by the fire alarm. 'Nurse!'

I emerged from my cubicle with staged, suspicious advances, the washroom hazy under much steam. The cubicle beside showed a forced lock, a speckled blood trail enticing my eyes to follow. Slumped into a corner, the old man spilled blood via his mouth, an accompanying gargle sounded like the final dregs escaping from a bathtub. The policeman knelt beside him, attempting to shift the man's considerable girth into the recovery position. I winced, averted my eyes, and then legged it.

Out on the ward, patients and clinicians mulled around, seemingly unprepared for a fire drill – despite my geriatric chic, I felt strangely inconspicuous. I looked downwards and walked on, a pair of Hush Puppies and a pair of plastic sandals passing without so much as a twitch toward the supposed felon. Glancing up, double doors stood not ten feet away – an escape so close.

'Ginger?' said a voice.

Fuck. Who? Me?

Brian stood opposed, sporting a silk dressing gown. 'Ginger, they wouldn't let me see you,' he said, hands on hips.

Not now, damn it! I fidgeted. 'You OK?' I said.

Brian sounded slightly choked. 'Are *you* OK, chuck?'

I nodded. *Nods don't count as lies, right?* 'Listen, I'm sorry for...' It was a relief to see him looking so alive and not-dead, but time was becoming precious. 'Well, I'm just sorry.'

Brian smiled.

'I need to go now. It's complicated, but I'll explain when I can. Please don't tell anyone you've seen me.'

A twitch to Brian's top lip suggested an urge to be nosy, though in the end he just nodded. 'Careful you don't run into the fashion police,' he said, looking me up and down.

I glanced over my loafers and shrugged. 'Like I said, it's complicated.'

'Well... see you then.'

'Yeh.'

A moment later I walked from the ward – it was simple.

Thirty-One

You've got it good, you
should thank up above.

Thinking logically, the police knew nothing of my intentions, and I was sure a particular girl's identity had remained elusive to them – at least for the time being. To find Ms Fish – and so the ring – I began in the most obvious place.

Approaching, the house was quiet. The exterior reminded me of a Lego manor house I'd built in the doctors' reception as a child – pristine, almost shiny, but just too faux. Ms Fish emerged from the front entrance, oblivious to me, dragging a large trunk across the drive. She appeared smartly dressed, more so than usual, as though she had a meeting with her bank manager and she rather fancied him. I was suspicious, and moved in.

'Something looks fishy,' I said. *Ha ha.*

Ms Fish looked up, seemingly unconcerned by my arrival, proceeding to wrestle the trunk into the boot of her Lexus. She straightened her appearance in the rear window and then clopped her heels to greet me.

'They let you out?' she said, her eyes surveying me.

I fidgeted. 'Sort of.'

'You look…' She abandoned the sentence and pulled a face.

I grunted and nodded towards her car. 'What's with that trunk thing? Off on a jolly?'

'Spain, actually.'

'What?'

Her expression appeared no more involved than informing me she was going to buy a pint of milk. 'My flight's this evening.'

'You're doing a runner?'

'I'm taking a sabbatical, Ginger.'

But what about the ring? What about the police? What about –
'What about *me*?' I blurted.

'I'm not quite sure what you're getting at.'

'Well I mean…' I felt my face flush and resolved to nudge the conversation forwards. 'Why the hell did you take that ring?'

She glanced away. 'I wasn't thinking.'

'Fuck. Really?'

Such an open exchange seemed to make her uneasy of prying ears – she scanned the street and tugged on my arm. 'Come inside.'

Ms Fish pulled me into the house, and from behind a tight blouse, our brisk pace made her chest jiggle. I tried to dispel the weakness of finding her so damn attractive. She settled me in the lounge, my bottom sinking so deeply in a soft leather armchair. The whole room was illuminated by a panoramic window which looked out over the garden – being as extensive and immaculate as I remembered. The chairs and sofa were a brilliant white that seemed to glow, the rest of the room littered with over-polished antique furniture and garish porcelain; for which Mr Fish must have quite handsomely funded the knock off Chinese reproduction trade. Ms Fish pulled open a drinks cabinet and poured herself a large measure of something.

'Drink?' she said, offering me a tumbler.

I pulled a face. 'Hardly the time.'

'Well, don't mind if *I* do.' She took a sip, her face creasing as though she were sucking a lemon. She observed the bottle and sniffed. 'Daddy's favourite – twenty years old. It costs a fortune. Tastes like shit.'

It was quiet for a moment.

'Why are you leaving?' I said.

'Isn't it obvious?'

'*I'm* not running.'

'So did the police drop you here?'

'That's not what I meant. I'm trying to sort things out.'

'Someone's dead Ginger. You can't just "sort" that out.'

Don't say his name, just don't.

'That noise, the blood...' She took a gulp. 'A hefty prison sentence looming over.'

'Maybe not.'

She looked away. 'It doesn't matter. I'm going away to clear my head.'

'Stay,' I said.

'No. I'd simply be dangling you a carrot.'

'It's not like that.'

'Yes Ginger, it is.'

'But we've been through...' *Who am I kidding? She's a stupid weakness, a cock tease – it's not like she even gives shit.* 'Well, I'm glad you were with me,' I mumbled. 'At least, I am now.'

She stopped me with a hard glare. 'Just remember – no blabbing until I'm mile high, mister.'

'What?'

'I had the wit to give a false name in A&E – it should have bought me enough time.'

'Jesus, you're so fucking selfish. I *will* talk to the police eventually.'

'Yes I'm sure,' she said, then sipping her drink. 'And I'll be several hundred miles away drinking sangria in the sun.'

'But—'

'So *then* you can tell them what you want – maybe that's truth. I don't care.'

'They'll still find you, a couple of hours on a plane is all it takes. In fact, maybe they're waiting outside, right now – all they have to do is check CCTV and—'

Ms Fish slammed her tumbler upon the cabinet. 'Fuck off, Ginger.'

'I can't,' I said, my voice deeper, more manly. 'Not until you give me that fucking ring.'

Opposed to me stood a coffee table, upon which a handbag had been discarded. Ms Fish nodded in that general direction. Tentatively, my hand delved inside and rummaged – the bag seemingly made from the skin of some kind of lizard – and amongst a miscellany of unknown objects, I clasped my hand around a small cuboid. The exterior felt like velvet and pleasured my fingers. I pulled back my hand, retrieving a small red box, and without hesitation I flipped it open. Inside, presenting to me like an autonomous marriage proposal, was a gold ring, my source of peril. The red stone caught the sunlight and twinkled – it was rather pretty, considering. I closed the box, slipped it into my pocket and was quiet. Ms Fish was staring into her glass, gently spinning it upon the cabinet.

'So this whole ring business,' she said, a while later. 'What's it about?'

'You heard the yarn, what it's worth,' I mumbled. 'The owner wants it back. Pretty badly.'

'Will you? Give it back?'

'Yeh, I think.'

'Meaning?'

'The bloke thinks he runs the Yorkshire Mafia from his chip shop, makes things a bit awkward.' I took a deep breath, stood up and shook away my thoughts. 'Anyway...'

Ms Fish offered me a glass, and as I nodded, she promptly

depleted the bottle by two generous measures. 'It sounds rather seedy,' she said.

'Seedy, undesirable, never-ending-torment – take your pick.' I agitated my drink with a circular motion and took a long sniff, alcoholic fumes tingled my nasal hair and made me sneeze. Still, the prospect of what lay ahead prompted me to down it in one – the drink projected across the room by a mixture of cough and splutter. 'Bloody hell!'

Ms Fish twitched, I think almost smiling. 'Like I said, tastes like shit.' Her eyelids appeared to be hanging lower, probably under one too many glasses of 'Daddy's favourite'. 'Want a smoke?' She flicked the lid of a gold cigarette packet, and as she leaned into the drinks cabinet, her stiletto heel caressed the stocking of the opposite leg.

'Not really,' I said, trying to dispel the taste.

She shrugged, raising her glass. 'To Spain,' she said, before taking a gulp and clasping a cigarette between her scarlet lips. 'Have you been to Spain, Ginger?'

'No,' I said, through a splutter.

'I love it – Daddy has a villa in the south.'

'Nice,' I mumbled.

She lit her cigarette via a matchbook that appeared to promote some exclusive hotel, and after puffing away the smoke, her tone was then dourer. 'I just have to tolerate Daddy's little slut.'

'Sounds cosy.'

'No. Not cosy at all.' She took a long drag, savouring and exhaling through the nose. 'Still…' Then, she let the cigarette drop, igniting the drink I'd spat out moments before, a trail of blue flame spreading across the cabinet. 'Fuck them.'

The fire followed the alcohol, spilling onto the carpet, and as my eyes caught up, I saw my loafers were aflame. 'Shit! Help me!' I blurted, stamping my feet about like Riverdance.

Ms Fish appeared weary, stepping back from the cabinet and glancing downwards. Lacking any shred of urgency, she doused my feet with tonic water, a strange combination of fizz and sizzle as the flames petered out. The shoes were scorched to a deeper shade of brown – had they not been on my feet, I would have applauded the incineration of such monstrous footwear.

Meanwhile, the drinks cabinet was ablaze.

'The bloody house is on fire!' I blurted, grabbing a cushion from the sofa and wafting at the flames.

She shrugged. 'Daddy won't need it.'

'What?'

'Fuck them.' She glanced away and finished her drink, a flicker of blue flame reflecting in the glass.

As the curtains caught alight, I realised my attempts as a firefighter were futile. 'Er, you need to call 999. Now.'

Ms Fish simply shrugged and made for the door, at which point her nonchalance caused my standard level of mistrust to increase, and I feared playing a pawn in yet another escapade.

'What's going on?' I shouted after her.

'Pardon?'

I manoeuvred quickly, standing over the door and holding it shut. 'I know you're up to something.'

'Excuse me,' Ms Fish attempted to shove me aside, but I remained steadfast, shrugging her off with a force that seemed to surprise her – and indeed myself. *You shall not pass!*

'Tell me,' I said. The smoke was thickening, rising, close enough to make us both cough. 'If you think I'm bluffing, think what I've got to lose. I've got nothing, fuck all but a date with a gangster who wants to rip out my throat. So if we go up in flames, I don't give a shit.'

I wasn't convinced that Ms Fish really believed I wanted to die, but her pupils had dilated enough to suggest she'd realised I was going to be awkward.

'We're going to cut and run,' she snapped. 'Daddy's business is fucked, he's practically broke. We're not coming back, the house isn't ours anymore.'

'What? Then why steal all that money?'

'Daddy knows, he always knew. We planned the robbery. We've just been biding our time, otherwise it would have appeared too obvious.'

'My job?'

'Gone.'

'When was you going to say?'

'I wasn't.'

'Fuck.'

Across the room, a bottle shattered and I looked over Ms Fish to see fire spreading across the ceiling and the drinks cabinet a display of blue-flamed pyrotechnics – the heat was intense.

'Ginger!'

We fled into the hall, almost galloping together as we made our escape, out through the front door onto the drive. Looking back, smoke followed our trail, flames inside the front window looking like Satan's snow globe – such swift ferocity was really quite something. I propped myself against the Lexus, catching my breath. Ms Fish stood beside, watching the house burn, but betraying no emotion.

Then, a while later she said: 'Maybe things will work out for you in the end.'

I smiled, careful to project sarcasm, and raised an imaginary glass to her. 'To not being killed, at least for the time being.'

She sniffed.

Never seeing her again seemed logically preferable, though emotionally questionable. I took a moment to steady my knees. 'I'll see you then,' I said.

'Probably not.'

I took a deep breath and walked away – newly jobless.

Thirty-Two

I'll tell you straight
and you listen hard.

I tried to clear my head by walking briskly, taking in long back-streets away from the hustle of shops and busy roads – though the lack of distraction amplified my feeling of hopelessness. The University of Hull stood not half a mile away – a splash of opportunity amongst post-industrial gloom. Consequently, the far-reaching terraces I wandered had been usurped of 2.4 children and divided into student dwellings. One house spilled its innards from an open first floor sash, a mash-up of indie music, a trombone, bottle clinks and giggling. The sound of such whimsy angered me, that kids could dip in and out of the city, steal an education and head back to Middle England before the shit stains had chance to settle. Why should *my* life be stained by an accident of birth? I looked down and walked more quickly, the simple greyness of the pavement made me want to scream, punch something. I pondered a change to the boundary sign – *Welcome to Hull. If you value your future, you'd better fuck off pretty sharpish.*

My eyes picked out a telephone box. Slightly skew-whiff upon the pavement, I imagined it had transported Doctor Who from a parallel dimension. Inside, I retrieved a scrap of paper from my pocket and recited the number as I dialled. The dialling tone sounded twice.

'Who is it?' said a man's voice, gruff.

I paused. 'Ginger,' I said.

'Good.' His tone was calm, restrained. 'Have you got it?'

'Yeh.'

'Where are you now?'

'A phone box… Who is this?'

'You don't know me.'

'Right… Well… I'm not about to volunteer for a kicking.'

'Chas ain't in the mood for games.'

I drew in a heavy breath. 'Let's get it straight,' I said, 'I hand over the ring and then walk away. Right? I just walk away.'

'I can't see a problem with that.'

'No funny business.'

'Dunno what you mean.'

'I want your word.'

'Can I get you on this number?'

'Like I said, it's a phone box.'

'Stay where you are, just for a bit. I'll call you back.'

'Hang on—'

He hung up.

A moment later, an old-school ring tone sounded – I answered immediately:

'Hello, it's Ginger.'

The voice was low, and hit me like a punch in the stomach: 'I had impetigo as a kid – that was about as difficult to get rid of as you.'

Such words elicited a Pavlovian fear, rendering me dumb.

'But like most irritations,' said Chas. 'I got rid of it in the end.'

I contradicted my dry throat to speak. 'I… I've got it.'

'So I hear.'

'You can have it!'

'You think?'

'You can have it right now.'

'I'll come get it shall I?'

'Right—'

'*Dickhead.*'

'Sorry! I didn't think. I'm sorry.'

'I hear a lot of sorrys kid – it's a word.'

'I don't want it. I never wanted it – it just happened.'

'A close associate of mine...' His voice cracked, as though his vast containment of anger had sprung an unexpected leak. 'He's not too good.'

'It was an accident.'

'*Really?*'

'Yes.'

'Like you ripping me off?'

'I wasn't! I just—'

'Save it.'

'But I want you to know—'

'Shut up.'

I was quiet.

'Get to the bus shelter on Walker Street – tomorrow night.'

'What?'

'Be there for six. Just wait. Someone'll see you.'

'But... I don't want anything to happen. I'm...' I spoke more tentatively. 'Sorry.'

'Do as you're told. Understand me?'

'Yes.'

'We'll decide what happens then.'

I paused. '*We?*'

'Be there.'

'OK.'

The line disconnected.

Thirty-Three

But you really disappoint, and
sometimes I just can't bear it.

Darkness settled. Like an over blanket softening the shapes beneath, you could squint and imagine the silhouetted council hovels to be Lower Manhattan. Four tower blocks stood aligned, monoliths seeming to await a ritual sacrifice. *Me.* As I elevated my gaze, I saw several windows glowing, some with no nets. Once, from a similar vantage point, I'd seen a topless lady close her curtains – but right then, God had to provide more than great tits to make me smile.

The particular concrete atrocity that Mum and Dad called home sported sliding front doors and a dead intercom, short-circuited by years of well-aimed urination. Such facts afforded me access with little more ingenuity than pulling the doors apart. I crept along the corridor, unnerved by the echo of my own footsteps, the laundry room fifteen loud paces to my right. I entered to a wave of heat that made me a little breathless. The vents had been reported on numerous occasions, though perhaps the blockage was an intentional effort at a DIY sauna. The large commercial washing machines were motionless and baring empty drums.

From a flat above, unimpressed Shania Twain warbled at volume, the bass creating a thud that reverberated around the innards of the machines, rattling them. I closed my eyes and slumped over a wooden bench. In spite of the slats grating my shoulder blades, the tension snarls in my muscles and Shania-fucking-Twain – I slept.

'Jesus Christ,' bawled a voice.

The noise destroyed my slumber, like a shattered mirror. I sat upright, my heart punching the back of my ribs. I saw Mum. I was pacified – a wholly new experience – if momentarily. The feeling gave way to a creeping unease. 'Shouldn't your swearing be more Muslim-friendly?' I said.

Her skinny arms went limp, allowing the washing basket she held to drop to the floor. 'What you done? You've been on telly, the lot. I ought to turn you in – you're a criminal.'

'I'm not!'

'Why you wanted by police then?'

I inhaled deeply, and again. To quantify the soothing properties of these deep breaths, I reckon I'd have needed ten-thousand gallons of air to be totally calm – and perhaps a little lighter fluid.

'Listen,' I said to Mum, turning her shoulders to make her look at me. 'I haven't done anything, whatever anyone says.'

'You've brought us shame. Your sister's beside herself. Syd's *dead*. The state she's in. Police came for you yesterday, said they'd be back. I pray you've nowt to do with it.' Mum held her head and looked away. 'Go hand yourself in.'

'I can't – I can't tell you why. But it wasn't my fault.'

It was quiet for a moment. I was usually astute in perceiving Mum's thoughts because of her predominant negativity, but the situation of pleading my innocence to murder was rather more intense than an argument over who ate the last Penguin biscuit, and the strain of her face made me think it was possible she had intricacies I had never given her credit for. I watched her forehead glisten, becoming acutely aware of the heat in the room and the moistening of my own body parts.

'You do believe me?' I said.

'Me and Dad had to come back – for *this*. If I don't believe you, it makes me…' She shook her head vigorously, as though to expel a poltergeist. 'I just don't know anymore.'

What did you know beforehand? How to cook a pizza in a frying pan? How to get four cuppas out of one teabag? Are we about to add empathy to the list?

My gaze settled upon the window, a small rectangular pane of chicken wire glass. It was light outside – light *grey*, that is. Beside a block of garages, a sapling stood supported upon a patch of brown grass. The twig showed little sign of flourishing – like every sorry bastard within two square, grey miles. And whilst pondering sorry bastards, I saw a prime specimen waddle by the window.

'Where's Dad off to?' I mumbled, wiping my forehead with my sleeve.

'Morning paper,' said Mum, her voice still bereft. 'Probably with your mug on the front page.'

Indeed – I wondered if I would even see the next morning. I wished I'd have woken up earlier, watched the sunrise, watched the milkman deliver methadone and hardcore VHS tapes; watched the graveyard shift dolies lurch toward the Jobcentre.

Still, fuck nostalgia – I craned my neck to watch Dad heave himself across the pavement. A marked police car turned into the street, pausing beside him.

'Police,' I yelped.

'What a surprise,' said Mum.

I saw Dad point back toward the tower block, toward the very window by which I spied on him. He frowned, appeared to speak briefly and then carried on his way. The jam sandwich moved in, spilling a uniformed officer. There was turbulence in my belly. I headed for the door, though quickly realised the corridor behind was merely a conduit to the front doors, to the advancing constabulary.

'Mum... *Hide me.*'

Mum glanced across the four corners of the room, then lit a fag with tremulous fingers. 'I won't be dragged into trouble,' she said. 'I've said it before, I'll say it again – hand yourself in.'

'For fuck's sake...' I crouched before one of the machines, poking my head into the drum, a stagnant whiff as I proceeded to fold my body inside.

'What you doing that for?' said Mum, her exhalation like a stuttering engine exhaust. 'It's just daft.'

The drum cradled me like a tin womb, more lovingly than Mum ever had. Such confinement created an echo, adding depth to my voice, making me sound less pitiable: 'If you let them find me, we're *all* done for.'

Mum spluttered, somewhat more vigorously than a usual fag fix. She took a couple of steps forward, tentatively, clamped the fag between her lips and then scooped an armful of clothes. She gave an unintelligible grumble as she pushed the clothes into the drum – the mucky sock pushed into my mouth was probably more accidental then symbolic.

I wretched.

A click, then creaking as the laundry door opened. Peering between a stale shirt and a screwed-up tabard, I watched the policeman breeze into the room.

'Mrs Jones,' he said. The tone was flat, as though vaccinated against a sense of humour. 'A word.'

Mum leaned against the machine door, closing it enough to obscure me – I peered stealthily through her Twiglet legs, sweating extensively. 'I wish you buggers would leave us alone,' she said.

'Funny time to be doing your washing,' said the policeman. 'Considering...'

Mum exhaled and gave a throaty cough. 'Considering what?'

'Your son, Mrs Jones. It's critical we find him. If you've heard anything, seen *anything*... It could be easy for lines of loyalty to become, shall we say, hazy. Just remember we need to speak to Lloyd concerning *very* serious crimes.'

There was a pause.

I imagined Mum's face tensing, making her look like a perturbed walnut. As her legs wobbled, I reckoned her thoughts would too. I mean, ten years previously, she'd shown no compunction in surrendering me to the corner shop for lifting Garbage Pail Kids stickers. Why the fuck wouldn't she give me up there and then?

Finally, I heard Mum say: 'Kecks'll get skiddies – an overblown game of hide and seek won't change that.'

The policeman's nosed twitched, it was small and pointy and stuck to his face like a carrot on a snowman. 'Where's Lloyd,' he said flatly.

"Scuse me,' said Mum. I saw her flick out a towel, allowing it to unravel and spread over the floor – it was a Smurfs beach towel. 'Prayer time,' she said, then stubbing her fag against the washing machine.

'That right? In the laundry?'

'Allah is everywhere,' said Mum – she kneeled over Papa Smurf. 'Privacy, please.'

The policeman stepped forward, wiping his boots on the towel. 'There's talk of Lloyd having an appointment later today.'

Mum stretched forward, lowering herself onto all fours and screeching what sounded like *Arabian nights* from *Aladdin*.

'Tell him to stick to that appointment.'

As I peered more intensely, the white of the policeman's shirt appeared dulled and his epaulettes wonky – as though stuck on with Velcro. He leaned forward, grasping beneath Mum's chin and pulling her head so she looked up to him. 'Are you listening, Mrs Jones?'

A feeling of doom swelled in my belly. I kicked open the door, emerging from the machine like a rabbit being smoked from its hole. 'Don't touch her,' I said, my voice almost a squeak.

'Well, well,' said the policeman, eyes widening. 'I think you'd better come with me, son.'

I shoved Mum to one side, grabbed the edge of the towel and tugged with all my strength. The policeman fell backwards, helmet toppling.

Crack.

As his head ricocheted from the bench, Mum shrieked. He rolled across the lino and vomited. His body jerked. He reached for purchase, hand skidding through the bile and chunk – he slumped. I grabbed Mum's arm, dragging her from the room like a caveman dragging an animal carcass to his cavewoman. Out in the corridor, I kicked the door shut, grabbed a broom from the cleaner's cupboard and jammed it tight between the door stop and the door handle.

I pulled Mum up from a crumple of bones. 'Go call the police,' I said, holding her shoulders to stop her trembling.

'You've killed the police!' she shrieked.

'He wasn't a policeman, Mum.' I couldn't help but shake her, perhaps hoping I'd dislodge some of her stubborn stupidity. 'And he's *not* dead.'

'What's happening to you? You're out of control. You're destroying this family. I dread to think what Dad'll say.'

I took a lung full of air, glancing away as I ushered her along the corridor. Out through the front doors, the cool air was sobering. I saw the cop car, saw the absence of a blue light and the faded decals. Be it a disposal or cheap mock-up, I'd been fooled only by my initial panic. 'Look.' Swivelling Mum, I pointed. 'Does that banger look like a real police car to you?'

She stared, but didn't reply. I reckoned her brain had fizzled, the cinders swept away by a caretaker called Incomprehension. I steered Mum toward the street, the car windscreen reflecting two forlorn looking figures – my clothes really were dreadful. 'Can you find me something to wear?' I said. 'T-shirt, jeans – something?'

Mum looked back, seemingly to gaze through my very existence. She touched her lip, twirling a tin wedding ring around her finger. We stood for a moment. Mum reached up and straightened my collar. It took three seconds, but if that moment had happened anytime during my childhood, I might have ended up at university.

She turned away, scurrying ahead in an old person kind of way. 'God help us… *Allah* help us. Allah help *you!*'

Thirty-Four

These fists are formed
with temperate hands.

I sat huddled inside the bus shelter on Walker Street, my eyes seizing upon the movement of every car, every person, every stray animal. For the sixteenth time that minute, I touched the ring box inside my pocket. Mum had brought me a hoodie and a pair of jeans – raided from a recycling bin – and for those moments my new clothes seemed to fit better than my own skin.

A black Jaguar turned into the street. The car seemed to exude a kind of conspicuous authority, creeping to a halt opposite. As the passenger window slid open, the face behind was familiar – Black Cab Man – his tracksuit top and unevenly shaven head at odds with the car.

I pulled back my hood, leaning in. 'Are we going for a ride?' I said, my voice tremulous.

'I'm here t'pass on information. That's it.'

I dug the ring box from my jeans and extended my arm into the car. 'Take it.'

The man appeared to recoil a little. 'Na. Not here.'

'But—'

'Go t'Infirmary, ward six, cubicle four.'

'What? Why?'

He pushed my arm away. 'Go.'

'Who do I look for?'

'Now.'

I snapped my arm back as the car moved away. What else could I do? I hurried off to the hospital.

I'd been waiting for five minutes, loitering beneath a 'no smoking' sign by the entrance to A&E. My hood hung loosely, protecting my identity with the façade of a Nike clad monk. The point was to conjure enough courage to face the unknown, to try not to die – for I feared pushing my luck. Taking a copious breath of evening air, I looked around. An ambulance took off in full light and sound, the shrill in my ears making me squint. A couple of young nurses trotted past, giggling – presumably not at me, though paranoia told otherwise. Lawless cigarette smoke drifted, the smell reminding me of Mum and seeming to pacify the cold, clinical atmosphere, if only for a few seconds. I fidgeted on my feet, grasped some decisiveness and ventured inside.

The queue for A&E greeted me with a medley of groans and blood stained dressings. I passed through, maintaining a brisk pace along a corridor and into the lift lobby. My gaze remained predominantly downwards, sporadic glances away from the ground prompting a tug on my hood each time I noticed a Big Brother camera. One of four lifts stood waiting, open for me – I acquiesced. Motion and fear combined to churn my innards like a lottery machine, the sixth floor arriving with an abrupt halt that made me shudder. As the lift door slid into itself, I controlled my breathing and walked onto the ward.

Disinfectant agitated my nasal hair, the gentle activity of early evening showing my entrance little concern. I found the door to cubicle four – closed tight. Obliterating any thoughts daring to probe my mind, I kept my momentum and entered without hesitation.

Chas.

The Chip Shop King sat upright, hospital bed his throne, prison denim as obvious as a stripy jumper and swag bag. Glowering, his pupils expanded into dustbin lids and I retreated from eye contact. Two men sat to a side, their epaulettes and clip ties like fancy dress – Screw #1 rose from his chair.

My mouth opened. 'Hello.'

'Get that hood off. No visitors here.'

'This is my nephew,' said Chas, voice cracking beneath a laboured affability. 'Cut us some slack, eh?'

'You're on remand – you know the rules.'

'Five minutes?' Chas yanked his arm, seeming to forget being cuffed to the bed. 'It's doing my nut in here.'

Screw #2 peered over his *Daily Mirror.* 'Guess that means you stop swallowing coins.'

'An unwanted guest in my Yorkshire pudding.'

'Spare us the spin, Holder. You fancied a jolly—'

Thud.

Screw #1 clobbered his partner with a drip stand. Screw #2 slumped into his *Daily Mirror*, face moulding to the paper like a chip shop Shroud of Turin.

Thud. Thud. Thud.

Screw #2 hit the floor.

Blood dribbled.

Then clinking.

I glanced up as screw #1 took the keychain from his belt, Chas flicked away his handcuffs and stretched from the bed into full beer barrel frame.

Don't look at me!

'So where's the *money?*' said screw #1, stood rigid, like a robot without a battery.

Money? Where's the fucking escape pod?

Chas gave a deep exhalation. 'You made the right decision, Terry.' His words were flat, no gratitude. 'But you know we need to make this look convincing?'

'The *money?*'

'Sorry, Terry.'

I'm sorry too... for too many 'maybe's and 'what if's... and I'm sorry for Syd... and for Ms Fish... I'm sorry for everything...

Chas caught screw #1 by the scruff, then holding him in a head-lock and squeezing, his face passing though deepening shades of red. There was no struggle, but a splutter, then a sense of resignation – inevitability even – as screw #1's face arrived at a raw purple.

Thud.

The tally of slumped bodies doubled.

The Chip Shop King shot a glance over my whereabouts. He approached, heal clipping screw #1's ear. His voice was abrasive, like striking a match. 'No fuss. Got it?'

My nodding was repeated and exaggerated. *I've got it. I really have got it... Does he know I've got it?*

As I backed myself into a corner, the door opened, and a fifth body entered the room.

Frankenstein.

That is, a full head mask. Yet the figure stood no more than five feet tall, slouching, hands in pockets and fumbling within baggy jog pants – a monster of disaffected youth.

'Bang on time,' said Chas. He slapped Frankenstein on the back, hard enough to elicit a whiplash action.

'Was watching – like you said.' The monster's pitch evoked an image of hairless testicles – he sounded about twelve. He pulled from his jog pants a Jaffa orange, holding it aloft. The orange showed a face, carved crudely – like a pumpkin having a stroke.

I took a step backwards. 'W-what's going on?' I said.

A waft of agitated air caused me to glance back. Chas propelled the drip stand towards my head. I shrunk into myself, hitting the floor in foetal position. A throbbing over my scalp seemed to weigh down my eyelids. The Jaffa orange rolled across my peripheral vision, a fixed grimace that ogled my very soul.

Then black.

I came to upon a hospital trolley – inside a lift. I could feel a hold across my upper arm, a pinch I reckoned like the onset of a heart attack.

'No fuss,' said Chas, his fat face moving over me.

I scrambled up, his grip on my arm held tight. My head was hurting, a haze to my thoughts as time suffered a lethargy. He pulled me closer, an intensity to our proximity. Indeed, I could smell his sweat.

Behind, Frankenstein commanded the lift, his finger aquiver.

'It's been a while,' said Chas, with all the affection one would show chicken pox.

I stuttered. 'I-I've brought it.'

I fumbled my pocket, my hand feeling like a JCB digger fishing for tadpoles. I held the swag at arm's length, Chas relaxed his grip, opening the ring box and observing keenly – I imagined the contents projecting a glow onto his face. His eyes were wide, like large 'six strike' marbles, suggesting the activity in his head was stimulating a rush of adrenaline – I feared any voice of reason was being actively asphyxiated. Such a stare would have silenced me, had the air not carried a whiff of my own death.

'Let me explain? Please?' I had little control over the sorrow-ridden tone that spilled out – I almost wanted to punch *myself* in the face.

The Chip Shop King clasped the ring into his hand and stood stout. 'It's all about respect. Get it? *Respect*. I've got a face to uphold.' He clasped tighter. 'I didn't ask for this. You think I want *this*?'

I'm not sure of the usual places guns and drugs and murder get you, but what did you expect? You're a bad person.

'My partner, my friend half dead.'

My friend is dead. That's dead by the way.

'Now I'm on the run – and *I* don't run from anyone. But we've got to be clever – live to fight another day.'

Chas lifted his arm, striking me with his outer hand. The force was strong enough to cause a sting, yet weak enough to preserve my teeth. Knowing Chas's aptitude for common assault, I felt this was an appetiser preserving my flesh and bone for the main event. Indeed, Chas then gestured to blow out his brains with a finger gun, nodding to Frankenstein, who fumbled at the lift panel, opening it up to show a convolution of coloured wires. Reaching into the cavity, he retrieved a rolled up towel, general clumsiness allowing the package to unravel.

A gun hit the floor.

Frankenstein was quick to point said weapon, breathing heavily into the mask. 'Don't move!'

Expecting a tap dance?

I'd realised the game really *was* up now. All that I had negotiated, manipulated since happening upon that fucking ring; the vestigial happiness brought by Ms Fish; the whole charade had reached an apex, an expendable fate – to be spent imminently.

The lift halted, the door concertinaed. We spilled out onto a storage floor like a very unenthusiastic conga line, myself under the duress of a gun. All around stood redundant beds, chairs, and assorted paraphernalia, an iron lung particularly conspicuous. I led the way, controlled by Frankenstein's gun digging into my spine. Across the landing we ascended a short staircase, crashing through a fire door at the summit. There we stopped, upon the roof of the hospital, fourteen floors high, in an open breeze. The sky was clear, a dark blue that was edging into night. My panoramic view of the city showed it illuminated, reaching far into the horizon, each bedroom-light a twinkle in the northern cosmos.

'Fire escape across the roof,' said Frankenstein, breathless, pointing the gun in a Hollywood 'freeze sucka' kind of a way.

'Good,' said Chas, then nodding towards me, almost nonchalantly. 'Better deal with *that* first. Be quick.' He seemed expectant, as though a reliable clairvoyant had informed the future, and such a future wouldn't dare mess with Chip Shop Chas.

The gun appeared to be in the hand of a convulsing epileptic. 'I'm not sure...' said Frankenstein. 'I mean—'

'Man up kid!' said Chas.

Or not. Not manning up is fine.

'Think you can play with the big boys? Well prove it.'

The gun wobbled. 'But—'

'Prove it!'

Facing me, Frankenstein clenched the gun tight, as though wringing the neck of his nervousness, his hand steadied just a little, he raised the gun to my head. Chas's forehead bore a sheen of sweat, his face taut, so very attentive.

This is it, isn't it?

This is it.

Oh heck...

I scrambled backwards, terror pumping hard inside my chest. The wind hit my face and elicited a tear.

'Wait, please!' I continued to edge backwards.

'S-stop there,' said Frankenstein.

I glanced over my shoulder, certain death fourteen floors below. My heel hit against a short wall edging the drop, and I stopped. Teetering from the edge of the building, from the edge of my mind – and as I looked back to face the gun – it appeared from the edge of my life; I stared blindly and waited.

Thirty-Five

I know kid you'll have your day,
just don't think that day is today.

Frankenstein's breaths were heavy, staccato, like a countdown of my demise. I brought him into focus. 'Let me say something before… just let me speak!' I blurted.

His hand twitched, the gun wobbled, but he said nothing.

I shouted over his shoulder, my eyes wide and unblinking as they latched onto Chas. 'I brought you the ring didn't I? Doesn't that say something?'

Chas held up the ring box, the red velvet exterior moist by his sweaty palm. 'You were up to no good. I know that.'

'I wasn't—'

'Don't lie!'

'OK. I'll work for you. I'd be good. I'll do anything.'

'You reckon?'

'You asked me, before.'

The Chip Shop King expanded his chest and moved in beside Frankenstein, the whites of his eyes seemingly wrapped in red liquorice bootlaces. 'You appealed to my corrupting nature.'

'So now?'

'Now you just don't appeal.'

'But...'

He tossed a comment back with little more feeling than a scrap of afterthought. 'Sing.'

'What?'

'Sing a song.'

'What!'

'Any song. Sing like your life depends on it.' He laughed, appearing pleased with the sound of his own voice – a bellow that made me feel pain.

'I can't...'

'Sing!'

'OK.' *That TV show? Made Dad laugh?* I grasped a tune from some dusty vault, and indeed sang – or at least made a noise – like my life depended on it. My soul seemed to be extricated via an ode to a place where everybody knew my name.

Before me, Chas and Frankenstein stood like some kind of Laurel and Hardy double act – though considerably uglier and without the jokes.

So what if I just take these two out? Run at them shouting and kicking and punching? The worst that can happen is I receive a bullet a bit earlier than the end of this fucking song.

Keep singing!

'Sometimes you...'

If I aim myself in their general direction, swing my arms and legs about, who knows what might happen... well, apart from being shot that is – but if that's going to happen... for God's sake, stop singing this song!

I screwed up my face and screamed: 'The ace of spades.' Abandoning deliberation, I opened my eyes, released a random scream and charged.

Arghhhhhhhhhhhh!

Seconds felt like minutes, Chas showing a wide eyed incredulousness. I could almost hear the cogs turn as his mind reassessed the next move. We collided. I ricocheted from Chas's stout stance, the impact winding me and sending me off on a trajectory, myself and Frankenstein a tangle of limbs upon the roof. My brain felt like a hamster inside a runaway playball, spinning, unable to grasp control. I kicked out for purchase, arriving at a vaguely upright stance. A snapshot of reality synced with my brain, I found myself astride Frankenstein. The struggle had fizzled, he felt limp beneath me, and as some kind of involuntary response saw me take the gun from his hand, he offered no fight to the contrary.

I took to my feet, stepping back, pointing the gun, desperate to summon some kind of badassed-motherfucking-attitude. 'I'll shoot,' I bawled.

Well that's what they say on TV. So why do I sound like a wet sheep bleating into the night?

Frankenstein stayed down, edging away with a backwards crawl.

'I'll shoot,' I repeated, a little less wet, but hardly leading man.

Chas took a step forward, and despite holding a gun, my Pavlovian response was to take two steps back.

'Just let me go,' I blurted.

Chas smiled, it appeared forced, like pulling back on a phimosed foreskin.

I stuck the gun a little further toward him, exaggerating the movement. 'I mean it.'

'Clever kid – you gonna shoot me with the safety catch on?'

Safety catch? What safety catch? Which bit's the fucking safety catch?

'Give it up kid.'

'Don't move. Just don't move.'

'You wanna talk?' Still, Chas came closer, the gun no more intimidating than a hairdryer. 'Settle this man to man?'

'Keep back.'

'You held a gun before kid? Reckon you can figure out how to use it?'

No...

I glanced at the gun.

And no.

Chas stood close enough to reach out and touch me – I took half a step backward, the final reserve of roof before a multi-storey drop into darkness. It was the same place on the roof and the same sense of impending death – the whole thing felt as hopeless as it had a minute before – and *I* was holding the bloody gun.

There was a shot.

My arm jerked upwards, the force trying to fling me up and away into the night sky. The noise was like a very loud and very round full stop, forcing me into a childlike disbelief, my eyes closing for a couple of seconds before I dared override the reflex:

I pulled the trigger? Well, I might have twitched, but... Fuck, what if I've killed him? I'm not the bad guy... OK, better open my eyes now. Ready? One... two... two and a half... three...

Upon first glance, Chas didn't appear dead, nor demonstrate any misadventurous loss of blood. *Woo-hoo! Well, kind of...* He stood before me, brow cut in two by an earnest crease, his hands held up in Al Jolson appreciation. I scanned down his faded prison denim, and upon the toe of his shoe the ring box rested conspicuously.

My body swayed, anchored to the roof by spasmodic feet.

'You called my bluff kid.' Chas spoke quietly and with precise pronunciation, a slight break in the chunkiness of his voice that suggested a trepidation I was quick to clock. 'But be clever, eh? No need to do anyone damage.'

Indeed, the gun was just a prop, a kind of mini nuclear deterrent that occasionally – and quite accidently – almost killed people. Not that Chas knew as much.

I pointed the gun with well-feigned vigour. 'Just go,' I said.

His fingers flexed, pointing to the sky and pulling his palms taut. I wondered which crease represented longevity, and if I could decipher such wrinkles, exactly how much life he had left. 'You want me to walk?' he said.

'Yes.'

'Turn around and just carry on?'

'Yes.'

'As easy as that?'

I shrugged. 'It *is* easy.'

'And then? How do I know you're not gonna put a bullet in my back?'

'I'm not *you*.'

Chas released a short blast of air from his nostrils, projecting a kind of incredulous indignation. 'Drop the tool... then I'll walk.'

I shook my head, slowly.

'No time for a stalemate.'

I controlled my breathing, in through the nose, out through the mouth. 'I'm not in a rush.'

'Think the filth are sat eating a donut? Feet up on the desk? They won't be long kid.'

'Not my problem.'

Chas gave a laugh, betrayed by the strain shown in his temporal veins. 'And you really believe that?'

'It's true.'

'Kidnap, murder—'

'All you.'

'All *us*.'

I shook my head.

'You're a part kid – get used to it.'

'*You* killed Syd.'

'Speak to my lawyer on that one...'

'*You*.'

'What's your beef? Forget he double-crossed you?'

'He didn't deserve to die. *I* don't deserve to...'

'Think you're worth a bullet?' Chas held me with unblinking eyes. 'Sensible thinking throws you over the side.'

'What?'

'Multi-storey drop, certain death – could look accidental.'

'Lucky I've got a gun.'

'You won't shoot me. You've not got it in you.'

'Yeh?'

He appeared to restrain a smile. 'We both know it.'

'Try me.'

He lowered his hands.

'Hands up!' I thrust the gun toward him.

Chas appeared unmoved, a grimace showing as he bent to retrieve the ring. Behind, I caught a glimpse of Frankenstein, a good ten feet away, head down, huddled. I wanted to do the same, hide away in my own embrace, happy in denial. Chas straightened, hijacking my centre vision as he clasped the ring box into his fist. He took a step forward, his eyes resurveying me. 'You've had your moment kid. Pass the tool.'

'I said hands...' I waggled the gun, though abandoned the sentiment mid-sentence. I might as well have been wearing a tutu – at least then he might have laughed himself to death.

Chas moved closer still, expanding his chest like a red faced, middle-aged Bruce Banner. 'Time to call it a day kid.' His arm extended to within a few inches, open hand expectant. 'Give it up and I'll let you walk – call us quits.'

That sounds... But you do have a habit of lying Chip Shop Chas...

'Deal?'

For fuck's sake, he's a villain, a cheat – a bad guy. I give him the gun and he'll do exactly what he was always going to do – he'll shoot me. And I don't want to die.

I shot Chas.

It was deliberate. The force pushed him into a backward stagger, his arm moving over his chest, hand clamping onto his shoulder. His posture became crooked, he looked back, eyes so wide they seemed to dominate an impossible percentage of his face. A shade of claret seeped from beneath his hand, overshadowing the blue denim at an unhealthy rate.

'Armed police. Drop the weapon and hold your hands behind your head.'

We were surrounded, all at once, a cock-sure display of weaponry pointing at...

Me?

'Drop the gun.'

My grip tightened, fear masquerading as defiance – the sight of a dozen policemen, seemingly kitted out for the end of the world – I simply couldn't let go of the gun.

Chas blurted over the repeated commands, a melodramatic stagger towards the firing squad. He pointed back to me with a finger that looked as though it had been dunked in raspberry jam. '*Him.*'

'*Last warning...*'

'Attempted murder of a prison officer. Attempted murder of *me.*' Chas's words were breathless and lacked composure – though still seemed to project an undertone that was carefully degrading. '*He* murdered Sydney Clough. He's scum.'

I closed my eyes so tightly, my being unanimously in favour of its preservation, yet control over my hands seemingly impossible.

Let go of the gun. Let go of the gun. Let go of the gun. Let go of the gun...

Such a simple action remained beyond my ability, and desperately scared, I concentrated all my strength into one final release. A paraesthesia spread over my muscles, it was strangely pleasant, slipping into my mind and creating a momentary delirium.

I relinquished control.

And collapsed.

In a second I felt a grip around my arm, tight. An upward force pulled on me, strong enough to cause a dislocation.

'You all right?'

My eyes opened, as though from a lengthy sleep. Briggs stood over me, sweaty and ruffled, two armed officers either side, their attention pointing at me.

I shrugged – it seemed so strenuous to formulate a reply. My eyes moved quickly, capturing the scene. Glancing downwards, I saw my hoodie sporting blood spatters, yet I could feel no pain, which I reckoned was good. The gun had vacated my possession, presumably contained within an evidence bag held within safer hands than my own – I reckoned this was also good. Across the roof, Chas was slumped, a fuss around him and a fair amount of the red stuff. The ring box had tumbled to the side of his feet, punctuating his blood stricken pose – the back of my eyelids proved a much more agreeable sight.

'I'm in trouble?' I muttered.

'Looks that way,' said Briggs.

'I didn't mean for… I'm sorry.'

'Someone's always sorry.'

I peered up at Briggs, his moustache in spite of his downturned mouth and curling upward like a hairy smile. The perception was transient and probably arising by me being slumped beside him – still *living*. I took a deep breath, exhaling so much stress and tension, my body feeling like jelly. 'What'll happen?' I said.

'You come with us. We'll get you cleaned up.'

'Right.'

Briggs's tone dropped. 'Then we'll have a chat.'

PART SIX

Thirty minutes later

Thirty-Six

There's no greater sin
than the mess I'm in.

'Charles Holder is dead,' said Briggs.

'What?' I said.

''bout an hour ago.'

The police had been firm, but not unkind, as they had moved me from the hospital roof to an interview room. It had been a bit of a whirlwind, with no time to think – I didn't *want* to think.

'Cardiac arrest,' said Briggs, standing, hands tucked into his trouser pockets.

I sat opposed, staring down at the table between us. A cassette recorder made sporadic squeaks, documenting the conversation for posterity. 'But he was alive when...'

'That's right, *was*.'

'I hit his shoulder.'

'Stressful business getting shot.'

'He can't be dead.'

'Dead as a dodo.'

My eyes darted around, in every direction but that of Briggs. Across the table, Johnson had kept quiet but for his name and rank, beside me, an empty seat had been reserved for legal advice.

'Thinking twice about a shyster?' said Briggs, catching my glance.

I shook my head – I may have been outnumbered, but my encounter with John Edmund had entrenched a feeling that all solicitors were cunts. As such, I had refused the duty 'shyster'.

Briggs pulled out his chair, relieving his legs from the physical statement of a terrible diet. He leaned towards me and gave an exaggerated exhalation. 'Manslaughter at best.'

I stared at the table.

'You know that means jail?'

'It was an accident,' I mumbled, though realised it wasn't quite the same as spilling sauce on my favourite shirt.

'I'm not convinced you'd hack it inside.'

'One accident...'

Briggs was quiet for a moment. 'And Sydney Clough?'

I closed my eyes so very tightly.

'Two accidents? I reckon you're a proper Mr Clumsy.'

For a while, the low hum and random squeaks of the tape machine became the loudest sounds in the ongoing demise of Ginger Jones.

'Listen, sunbeam,' said Briggs, taking a breath. 'The best thing you can do is let *me* help *you*. There's nowhere to go from here, right?' He leaned in, holding me with unblinking eyes. 'No running, no hiding – and there's no-one to be scared of. He's dead.'

'But...'

'Come on sunbeam. Show some sense. Tell me what happened.'

So what's left for me? A prison cell? Yet more loneliness? The guilt of knowing... 'Fine,' I said flatly.

Briggs nodded, his pupils expanding into the brown of his eyes and suggesting he was rather more excited over the mess inside my head than procedural composure would allow. 'Good lad,' he said.

Good? Hardly. Maybe once. But not now. Not after...

I felt my eyes glaze, Briggs's face blurring as his moustache curled into a half smile.

'All right?' said Briggs. 'Take a deep breath.'

I did, and then another. It helped.

Briggs let me be for a few moments, though his foot tapping beneath the table betrayed a certain eagerness. Before long, and after further perfunctory enquiries concerning my well-being, a clear-plastic evidence bag was placed before me. 'We'll start with this,' he said.

Inside was a red velvet box – I knew inside that box was a ring.

'No rush,' said Briggs. 'All in your own time.'

So, I took another deep breath.

And I told the truth.

Thirty-Seven

I shouldn't waste my time.
I shouldn't waste my breath.

A long thirty seconds passed before my call was answered.

'Mum?'

The line crackled a little, though was otherwise quiet.

'Mum? It's me.'

I heard a breath, short, slightly clogged – it seemed almost a gasp.

'What you want?' said Mum.

'I'm with the police.'

'Right.'

Again, it was quiet but for her heavy breathing.

'I just want... to say...' The power of articulating my thoughts was seemingly lost. 'I mean...'

'What?'

'I'm sorry,' I blurted.

'I can't...'

'Mum?'

'I don't know. I just don't know.'

'Whatever happens…'

'I'll put Dad on.'

'Mum. Wait.'

She didn't and the line fell silent.

A few moments later, Dad said: 'What you want?'

Again, I was flummoxed. 'I… I dunno…'

'So why you callin'?'

'I just…'

'You've upset Mum. All this bloody carry on. What you playing at?'

'It's not…'

'Not what?'

'What it seems.'

Dad delayed his reply, though soon proved his moment to think had been misspent: 'Seems like you're up shit street,' he said.

Like I expected anything different from you. Fuck what did I expect? Why am I even talking to you?

'You still there?' said Dad.

'Yeh.'

'Right.'

My words rode upon a long exhalation. 'Don't think I care anyway.'

'What you mean?'

'Dunno – thinking out loud .'

'Well… whatever's happening, needn't drag us into it, eh?'

'Guess not.'

'Let us know how you get on.'

'Fine.'

'See you then.'

'Yeh.'

Dad hung up.

Thirty-Eight

Can't think what I've done,
don't know what I think.

A night in the cells is not actually unpleasant – at least not in the simplest context. Contrary to popular opinion, the food is average, the spaces are warm and the beds are not entirely uncomfortable – even the sporadic company of an officer checking to see that I wasn't dead had mitigated my sense of isolation somewhat.

I was, however, the master of my own torment. My mind worked through a cycle of apology, sorrow and denial, though whenever I tried to release, it appeared my thoughts were as equally incarcerated, bouncing around the cell and returning to my head with a stronger poison. It was futile.

'All right sunbeam?' said Briggs.

The inspector's voice was a rescue from my musing, yet as I lowered my arms and averted my gaze from the inside of my hands, I saw him filling the doorway like some kind of rotund bottle-stop – and my torment did not feel mitigated.

Briggs winked. 'Nice morning eh?'

I'm living in a fucking cell.

'Right then, I'll get to the point – we're giving you bail.'

Sorry, for a moment there I thought you said... 'What?'

'You can leave this morning.'

This elicited several palpitations. 'But...'

'You're not off the hook like – there'll be conditions, and we'll need you for a second interview.'

'But you said, before...'

'I know what I said sunbeam.'

'People are dead.'

'You making a case for the CPS?'

'How am I supposed to... I mean, after all this.'

Briggs moved in, the mattress collapsing like a sinkhole as he parked himself upon the bed beside me. 'Listen,' he said, breath confirming the recent consumption of an onion based snack. 'Holder was overweight and he lived a stressful life. He was never more than a packet of crisps ahead of a heart attack.'

'But I shot him.'

'It's a plausible self-defence.'

My hands clutched at the mattress, the walls seeming to close in and clamp my head like a vice. 'I can't live knowing... I can't be out on the streets. It's not allowed. Not after...'

'Yeh, well. I should tell you something about that, sunbeam.'

'What? About what? It's all a mess. What more to say? Eh? Syd is dead. Chas is dead.'

Briggs shrugged. 'Not exactly.'

'What?'

'Holder's not...'

'Not?'

'Well...'

'What you saying?'

'We needed the truth.'

I caught a gist, and that gist made me nauseous. 'You mean?'

Briggs glanced away.

'He's not dead?'

He inhaled through his teeth, creating the soundtrack of a tuneless whistle which elicited the memory of a long ago TV theme tune and the capers of a skinny, beret-wearing buffoon. Briggs then looked back towards me with a straight face that was in no way apologetic and more suited to a maverick American cop show. 'Let's just say Holder's not well,' he said.

'I fucking shot him.'

He took a lazy breath. 'Holder *did* take a turn. The cardiac arrest is bona fide, he's just not dead. We economised the truth 'cos we needed the truth.'

'You don't get it, do you?' I mumbled.

'Eh?'

'He'll still kill me!'

Briggs's reply was almost nonchalant. 'Doubt it sunbeam.'

'You can't stop him.'

He sniffed. 'A middle-aged overweight wannabe gangster?'

'Then how did I get *here*?'

'Like you gave us a chance.'

'But—'

'Think we could have done anything knowing scraps of a bloody story, eh? Mixed in with a few fibs?'

Reasonable thought had vacated the premises, I just stared at Briggs.

'We know the truth right?' he said.

I nodded

'Then you'll be fine.' He made to stand, grinning, his moustache tickling his top teeth. 'Anyway, he's not exactly gonna be leaping from his ITU bed.'

'Really?'

'Course he aint.'

I huddled into myself. 'Can you promise that? In blood?'

As Briggs stood, so he released the mattress from its constriction and I imagined the bed gasping for air. 'No need sunbeam.'

I remained unconvinced.

'Now,' he said, his tone altogether more cheerful. 'PC Smith here'll take you to see the custody sergeant – to cross your "I"s and dot your whatnots.'

I glanced across the cell to see a uniformed officer by the door – I was oblivious as to how long he had been there. I felt oblivious to *everything*.

'Just one more thing, sunbeam,' said Briggs, Columbo style. 'Any idea what Big Tits did with the cash? Lot of money to stick in a suitcase.'

'Er...' *Well Inspector, a chunk of it's still hidden in my*— 'No,' I said.

He paused for a moment, before the bush covering his top lip curled into a grin and he appeared satisfied. 'Right. Stay out of trouble then, eh?'

I nodded.

Briggs then left.

And, apparently, I was free to go.

One month later

Thirty-Nine

See you Ginger, now don't
you leave it too long.

I sat at the back of the chapel, a whole row to myself. I was some way from the other people, wailing and howling as they did – I was avoiding Mary, my sister, in particular. It was all so very black – too bloody black – except for me that is. I wore my one and only work shirt, a pale red derived from white cotton, a vivid sock and a recent ninety degrees cycle wash. I probably looked like I'd just finished a shift at McDonalds, but as I say – I was at the back.

So, to remember a person for whom I had little respect and often hated – Sydney Clough, as the minister called him.

I hadn't missed Syd at all really, by the simple fact it was too uncomfortable to think he was dead. I kept thinking he'd turn up on my doorstep with a stash of porn at a reasonable price. If I'd *really* thought him dead I think I might have cried. Maybe.

'... loved by friends and family,' said the minister.

I didn't hate Syd anymore. Like lots of things – it just didn't matter.

His mum was at the front, wailing in harmony with Mary. Syd had been in and out of foster care as a kid; his mum a wino, and his dad a myth of affluence for whom she'd compromised herself after a David Bowie concert. She was crying – but I couldn't help think she just liked the attention.

'We remember with affection, for happy memories live forever in our hearts, they make us smile,' said the minister. 'Still, Sydney makes us smile.'

For a time, Syd and I had been one another's only friend – good friends – and I wouldn't forget that. But I wanted to scream at the futility of his life. It seemed so sad that we could only honour him in death, *because* he was dead. I supposed Syd was an inspiration – to *do* something.

'We now turn to page fifteen in the blue hymn book – *All Things Bright and Beautiful*,' said the minister, 'one of Sydney's favourites.'

I smiled to myself. The only music Syd ever liked was about niggers, guns and big assed booty bitches. I doubted he'd ever set foot in a church.

The people stood as an organ began to play, talent-less fingers making it sound like bagpipes – it was horrible, and my moment to leave.

So, I said goodbye to Syd under my breath and slipped away unnoticed.

Forty

What's your
beef? I'm no thief.

'Three grand!' said Dad, huffing and puffing, descending the steps from the Magistrates' Court rather tentatively. 'How can that be right?'

'It's the law, Morris,' said Mum, her arm clasped around Dad's, almost like a care assistant. Both appeared to have made a modicum of effort, Mum in a long floral dress that looked like it had been dug-up from 1973; Dad sporting his wedding and funeral suit, which, since its last outing, appeared half a pork pie short of exploding.

'The law's bollocks,' said Dad.

'Let's get fish and chips, celebrate that it's all done and dusted.'

'How can it be? I've gotta pay back three bloody grand.'

I stood to the side of the steps, a well-placed bush halfway down affording me a stealthy view – Mum and Dad couldn't see me, and I didn't want them to.

'Dance with me, Morris,' said Mum, halting their descent and grinning.

'What?'

'Like the old days.' She dropped a step, spun rather creakily on her heel and looked up at Dad. 'Go on,' she croaked, tickling his belly and seeming to create some kind of tidal shift though his girth.

'Give over woman.'

Mum held Dad in a bear hug, emulating the kind of slow, grope-laden dance that happens at the end of a school disco.

'You on bloody heat or what?' Dad wriggled about, though his attempts to shake her off were rather feeble.

As Mum pinched his bum, Dad jumped, obesity and gravity working together to pull him from her grapple – he fell the remaining few steps like a keg of beer on a barrel drop.

'Morris!' Mum screeched.

Dad was a heap at the foot of the steps. I almost rushed to his aid – but I'd travelled by bus, and it was due in five minutes.

So I left.

Forty-One

The choice is yours. Don't
let your life go wrong.

The sun shone through the office window, making me squint. Outside it was cold, November, and practising for winter. Inside, double glazing had accentuated the direct sunlight and was making me uncomfortably hot. I undid my top button – I hated the sun for trying to fool me into thinking it was a nice afternoon.

I was back at work.

'OK chuck?' said Brian.

I grunted. 'That Donna on packing row two just pinched my arse.'

'Really?'

'Outside the bogs.'

'Well you are our little hero.'

'She stinks.'

'Another broken heart.' Brian studied his magazine closely. 'Suzi Star says that Cancerians – you – "must not think that because things have always been a certain way that they have to stay like that forever. Change is possible". What d'ya think?'

I paused. 'Only girls and gayboys read that shit.'

Brian peered over his magazine. 'Meow!'

I flopped into my seat and put my feet up on the desk, on the floor, then back on the desk. Change wasn't just possible, it had become a necessity.

'It's the line dancing final tonight,' said Brian. 'You coming to cheer us on?'

I shook my head and fiddled with a fish shaped eraser. 'So who *are* these new owners anyway?'

'Administrators. They'll just want a quick sale, pay off creditors – won't give a toss about *us*.'

'Neither did Mr Fish.'

'Not quite the same thing, chuck.'

'I didn't realise there were subtle grades of not giving a toss.'

Seemingly in recognition of the cantankerous taint to my tone, Brian moved on with the conversation. 'I still can't believe you covered for the little fish – and for all that time.'

I shrugged. 'Truth's out now.'

'For what good it's done. I ask you – British justice! And I hope those other bloody brutes rot in hell.'

'Don't remind me.'

'But you're a hero.'

'They're not actually dead, remember.'

Brian pulled a face. 'Then they should rot behind bars!'

I cut my thoughts and continued with a more dourly voice. 'My dad was up in court yesterday.'

'Oh?'

'He's got to pay back three grand.'

'Well I suppose that's good?'

'Kind of. Only thing is he fell down the steps outside the court – apparently he's broken his leg in three places.'

'God. I'm sorry.'

'Well, at least now he's got a *real* reason to claim disability.'

'If you want to look at it that way.'

'Mum was all over him too – it's like they've never been apart.'

Brian shrugged and stuck his face back in his magazine. 'And so the natural order of the world is restored. We can all get back to normal now, eh? Let's look forward to the millennium bug annihilating humanity.'

I paused. There wasn't a normal anymore – not for me. Normal was driving a scooter beneath the city, plotting an abduction, defiling a beautiful lady. Maybe the old normal was still there, somewhere; but I couldn't see it – I didn't *want* to see it.

'Brian?'

He didn't look up from his magazine. 'Yeh?'

'I've got something to say.'

'Go on then, chuck.'

'It's time for change.'

'That's the third time this afternoon.'

'Now.'

'Can't you wait until after tea break – I brought us both a bun.'

I stood up. 'See you Brian.'

He didn't move as I passed him. 'You coming to line dancing tonight then?'

I looked back briefly, then kept walking.

All the way to the kettle. I switched it on. 'You know what Brian?'

'What's that?'

I smiled. 'I'd love to come.'

Forty-Two

Maybe it's today I ride
my horse into the sunset.

That afternoon, I left work early, taking a bus across the city – and perhaps existence felt a little less futile.

I stood before a fairly inconspicuous house. It was bright outside, but bloody cold, and trotting up to the front door, I shivered. The doorbell made a sound like a bad game of *Operation*, and a man was keen to answer.

'You Ginger?' he said. His tone was polite, though he was unshaven and smelt of sweat.

I nodded.

'Come on through.' He grinned and held the door open. 'Out the back fella.'

I stepped inside, a little cautiously, and he directed me through a messy house. Out the back, the fenced-in garden contained a hoard of old washing machines, spare wheels, a kitchen sink and similar presumed scrap. There was a patch of green grass, uncontaminated by the rubbish around.

And there she stood.

My hands were cold as I pulled from my back pocket a clipping from the local trade mag and compared her to a picture I'd circled in biro. She was a GS Vespa, metallic blue and cream, a little worn, but beautifully so.

'Like I said,' the man mumbled, 'she needs a bit of attention.'

I bent my knees and felt underneath. 'Some rust down there.'

'She's still a good runner.'

'How much then?'

'Well the advert says…'

I sniffed, but didn't look at him. I wanted her, I was sure of that. Straightening up, I faced the man. 'Bit much.'

'I'll knock off a tonne, but that's it. It's for the kids you see – I wanna take 'em to Florida.'

'I've got cash.'

As I pulled a sandwich bag from my underpants, the man pulled a face. 'Strange place to keep it,' he said.

'It's kind of a habit,' I said, tugging on the seal. 'So how much again?'

'Like I just said…'

I grinned. 'Deal.'

The Preston Straight was a road, so called by its lack of curvy characteristics, popular with hairy bikers keen on speed and the seeming anonymity of the countryside. I commanded my new Vespa along this road. The sound of an overactive hairdryer sustained under my twisting of the throttle, a noise that resonated across the countryside. The wind chill made my teeth chatter, my fingers so cold I practically lost sensation – but I was happy. I was happy to feel the open air; hear the buzz of the engine; see the fields whizz by. My wheels consumed the road, with each twist of the throttle and each acceleration, I felt totally in control. It was a feeling I'd forgotten, indeed, I'd known little of. But I liked it. I smiled to myself.

Epilogue

The Lion Hotel Line Dancing Quintet finished sixth (out of six) in the regional dance finals, losing on account of a technicality: They were crap.

HOLDER, Charles. Passed away at the Royal Infirmary on 30th November aged 50 years, loving husband to the late Samantha, much loved dad and granddad. Service to be held in the Small Chapel, Chanterlands Crematorium on Thursday 12th December at 10.30am. Flowers welcome but donations to Dove House Hospice may be left at the service.

HOLDER, Charles. Dad, you're with the angels now. My heart is broken, I will miss your big hugs so much. Love you forever, Cindy. XXX

Night night Granddad, love Shane and Brittney. XXX

HOLDER, Charles. Dear brother of William, in-law Pauline. Still can't believe you're gone. Miss you loads mate. Love Billy, Pauline and the girls.

HOLDER, Charles. A good friend that will be sadly missed. Sympathy to Cindy and family. Rest in peace – Arthur Long (Longie).

HOLDER, Charles. Never forget the way you looked after me when there was no-one else. Will miss you 'Uncle Charlie'. Leon.

HOLDER, Charles. Sadly missed. Rest in peace son. Mum.